# of Forgiveness

A NOVEL

CANNIO CARDOZO

BlueRose ONE .com
Stories Matter
NewDelhi • London

BLUEROSE PUBLISHERS
India | U.K.

BlueRose ONE.com
Stories Matter
NewDelhi • London

For permissions requests or inquiries regarding this publication, please contact:

BLUEROSE PUBLISHERS
www.BlueRoseONE.com
info@bluerosepublishers.com
+91 8882 898 898
+4407342408967

ISBN: 978-93-7310-569-7

Cover design: Yash Singhal
Typesetting: Namrata Saini

First Edition: January 2026

Acknowledgment

First and foremost, I thank Almighty God for His abundant blessings and guidance throughout my writing journey.

I am deeply grateful to Rev. Fr. Silvestre D'Souza, Provincial Superior of the Karnataka-Goa Province, and to Rev. Fr. Alexander Braganza, Provincial Delegate to Canada, for their encouragement. My sincere gratitude is extended to Rev. Fr. Steny Mascarenhas and Rev. Fr. Jeevan D'Almeda for their constant support. I also wish to express my special thanks to Jennifa Cardozo for providing constructive feedback.

Finally, my heartfelt thanks go to BlueRose Publishers for their valuable assistance in bringing this work to publication.

Contents

Part I

Part II

Part I

Chapter 1

All Souls' Day

The saints had returned, and the souls arrived. Maria's soul yearned to be a saint.

'Will they forgive me?' A question popped into her mind.

The sun had set on All Saints' Day, and the day dawned on All Souls' Day. The church bells had yet to ring to wake the faithful for the Mass.

It was still a calm morning. The first alarm to wake the seniors in Goa had not yet arrived. *Ponkpank!* The alarm of the *poder* (horn of the bread man) woke people up even before the rooster's crow. Maria hadn't slept a wink that night. She rolled over and over in her bed. Her mind was preoccupied with the early Eucharistic service on Soul's Day, which she had to attend. Finally, she opened her eyes; it was still dark outside beyond the window. In the darkness of her own room, she felt for her glasses and grabbed them from the nightstand. She switched on the lights, closed her eyes, and joined her hands. As usual, she sat on the edge of the bed. Unlike other days, she wasn't drowsy while praying.

Later, she yawned and stretched her hands. Dragging her legs, she walked through the sitting room, dining room, and ended up in the kitchen. Her house was nothing special. The most expensive items were a gramophone and a manual Singer sewing machine, with which she earned her livelihood. The walls of her house were too high for her small stature, and hence had become the best place for lizards and spiders' night parties. However, for flies, it was a death trap. Although her dwelling was dusty and rusty, on that day, it suffused the aroma of cooked pork and pumpkin dishes.

She sipped her tea in the kitchen every day, unfailingly. She knew she was addicted; she couldn't say no to it. Her mind could think of nothing else but being forgiven. It was a sign of old age. Maria, born in the late 1930s, grew old in Goa, the 'Rome of the East' in India, which was then a Portuguese colony. She was proud to be a Goan Catholic, and, being the eldest of the four siblings, was expected to be a paragon of virtue and a living saint.

After tea, she finished all her morning activities in haste, and at the entrance of the closed door of her house, she sat on a chair. Resting her hands on her walking cane, she waited to be picked up for Mass. Anxiety draped her mind, and a cotton sari draped her body. She got up and walked to the window every now and then. With spectacles on her wide-opened eyes, she looked through the window towards the bushy front garden. She had not heard or seen anyone walking on the cemented brick pathway towards her house. She turned to look at the antique pendulum clock placed above the calendar, which had been given to her as a compliment. Every tick made her heartbeat rise. She almost thought she would be late for Mass. Head down, she moved towards the altar and picked up the Holy Bible from the drawer of a table. Flipping through the pages, without paying attention to any verse, she removed the hundred-rupee note.

A knock on the old-style double-folding door made Maria rush. She immediately pushed the hundred-rupee note into her sari's blouse. She placed her hand over her face and paused for a while before the second rhythmic knock. Biting her lips, shaking her head while taking deep breaths, she opened the door. Dressed in formal attire, her grandson entered. Instantly, his taste buds tuned to the aroma surrounding the house, and he was in seventh heaven.

He said, "After returning from Mass, I will leave only after the food you cooked in the kitchen is finished."

Maria, while covering her hair with the black veil, said, "No! The food is not for you; it's for my father."

His brows drew closer, his face tightening as he retorted, "What! For your father? Before my birth, you gave him the Big Adios!"

Maria, holding the cane in one hand and the other hand clenched into a fist, said in a gravelly voice, "This modern generation will never understand our exclusive Goan Catholic tradition on All Souls' Day."

He placed his hand on her shoulder and, in a soft tone, said, "Nana, you always do this. You don't share your life experiences with others. That is why people in the vicinity don't feel comfortable talking to you. Why do you always swallow the truth and cut a poor figure before others?"

Grumbling and gently biting her lips, she said, "You can think whatever you want, but right now, I can't tell you. We might be late for Mass."

He tenderly placed his hand on her hand holding the cane and said, "Gone are the days when you walked to the church. Now, by car, we can reach within five minutes, so we still have twenty minutes to spare."

Maria ignored, turned a deaf ear to him, and continued, "I am carrying some money with me to purchase flowers and garlands to decorate my father's grave. That will definitely take time, so we should leave now."

He replied, "Nana, don't worry about it. We can fetch them after Mass, on our way to the cemetery. By then, most florists will be open."

Maria ambled to her rocking chair. Taking a deep breath, she said, “Ok, ok, let me tell you what happens on All Souls' Day. It's a day of freedom for all the souls in purgatory. The evening before, we cook the food that our loved ones liked and leave it for them. Some leave it in the utensil itself, while others leave it on the house roof. We believe the souls come and eat the food.”

In an uncertain tone, he asked, “Do they finish the food kept in the utensil?”

“I am not sure, but I know it always remains there, and we eat it after 3:00pm. That is the time the souls return to the place they come from. It is assumed that the food on the rooftop is eaten by the birds."

“Nana, one thing I don’t understand: why did you only cook what your father liked?”

She inhaled deeply and replied, “My father drank like a fish. He fought with and used abusive words against my mother. At times, he even pulled her hair and coerced her into giving him money to drink. My mother always said ‘Feni (cashew fruit liquor) set our house on fire’"

“What are you saying, Nana? You mean Feni is the cause? People earn their daily bread through it. Every tourist likes it, and it’s a speciality of Goa.”

Shifting her cane to the other hand, Maria said, “Yes, I completely agree with you. However, when you have your own cashew plantation, you have no limit for Feni.”

“You mean to say that your father was not a good man, is it?”

Nodding her head, she said, “Yes, he wasn’t, and he requires our prayers for his purification. I believe that on this All Souls’ Day, he will be freed and will come to visit our house.”

After a pause, he said, “Grandma, I think we can make a move now, and maybe I will come here today for dinner.”

“That sounds good.”

Maria caught her grandson's hand and stood up to put on her footwear. They came out onto the balcony. The left side of the cement sofa on the balcony had two jasmine flower pots. Maria gently touched the flowers, slanted them towards her nose, and sniffed them deeply. She wiped her tears with her sari *pallu.* The grandson locked the door, turned to hand over the keys, and laughed, saying, "Oh, the souls not only eat inside but also play mischief outside. Ha ha! It seems Grandpa has placed the pots from the garden on the balcony." Maria turned and looked into his eyes. Her red, watery eyes turned his laughter into a soft voice. He asked, "What happened, Grandma?"

With a slack expression and with dull, wet eyes, she said, "I know it's a joke for you to move these pots from the garden to here."

"But, Grandma, you know, every All Souls' Day, we play pranks by hiding or moving the things that are outside the house."

"Yes, I know, but my husband liked and placed these flowers at the altar. Their fragrance made our house a cozy home. He loved and believed in Jesus until the end of his life. A gem of a person and the salt of the earth are the best expressions to describe him. Here on earth, I don't pray for him, but I intercede through him to pray for me. I did it yesterday on All Saints' Day."

With a downward cast face, he said, "I am very sorry."

"You need not be sorry. I should be sorry, for I will never be a saint and be with my husband eternally in heaven."

"Grandma, even at this age, you attend Mass and do all your prayers faithfully. Then why will you not go to heaven?"

"Yes! I do my best, and I have even forgiven them, but will they forgive me?"

He caught her hand and, while taking her down towards the steps, said, "I don't know who they are. However, I am sure God will show mercy on you and will take you to heaven."

Maria buttoned her sweater to stay warm in the chilly morning. The surface of the earth was damp from the dew, and even the tiny spider webs were visible. Looking at them, Maria felt that nothing remains hidden in the sight of God. The truth about her life will come to light, one day or the other. The morning welcomed them with the sounds of birds chirping and roosters crowing at the top of their lungs. From the moment Maria had woken up, she had waited for the rooster to announce the good news of the new day. But now, Maria hoped to receive forgiveness in order to be with her husband in heaven, eternally. Maria sat in the car with a gloomy face, for, just a while before, memories had reopened old wounds. People often said that the love she received from her late husband was eternal and that they were a match made in heaven. However, even after death, they don't meet in heaven, then where?

Chapter 2

Shammai's Days

"Shuuu! Who's that? I guess I know who you are. What brings you here?" Maria screamed at the neighbour's daughter, Kia. Maria was known as *Shammai* (grandma) throughout the village. "It's already three o'clock noon, and all souls have returned. What brings you here? This is not the time to play pranks—you should have done that yesterday," *Shammai* said with a stern voice.

In the afternoon, when the sun hovered in the sky, *Shammai* liked to play hide-and-seek with its rays. She kept score each time she managed to successfully escape its harsh rays. Sitting in her shady, cozy backyard, she fought the refreshing diurnal breeze that hindered her attempts to thread a needle with her feeble, trembling hands. She was so engrossed in it that even a football-sized flying disc that bounced and spun into her courtyard could not steal her attention.

Kia, the young lass whose eyes were hidden beneath the curls of her dark hair, had hopped over the old wooden hedge with her loyal dog, Leader, to fetch the disc. They landed in a heap with grass glancing out from beneath the carpet of crackling, parched leaves, smiling at the sunlight. Amidst this untrimmed plot of land, Kia saw *Shammai*—a gray-haired lady, her tapering eyes sunk deep amidst the wrinkles that decorated them—concentrated on the nib of the thread and the eye of the needle. Kia tiptoed like Tom the cat, trying to avoid the attention of Jerry in the cartoon series.

"Yes! Shuuu!" Those were the words hurled at Kia when she was caught red-handed, just as she was about to stretch her tiny fingers to pick up the flying disc in *Shammai's* compound. Startled, Kia froze and couldn't utter a word. First, it was the articulation of the unanswered questions; now there were words of command.

"Don't you have the courtesy to help an old woman like me?" Kia's face turned pale—she felt like a bird without feathers. She got a little closer, only to face stern reply: "Take this needle and thread it." Kia softly called for Leader.

"Who is the leader here? I am the leader!" *Shammai* snapped.

Kia, with a trembling voice replied, "Leader is my dog."

"Forget about him for now—take this," *Shammai* said, forcing a fake smile while Kia, with her heart pounding, threaded the needle. As soon as she accomplished the task, a complaint emerged from *Shammai*, raising a brand new jean.

"Look at this pant—torn in the middle! How could anyone sell it to my beloved grandchild, who looks nothing less than a model? Here I am, spending my time and energy in stitching it!"

Perceiving *Shammai's* ignorance, Kia couldn't hold back her words. In a soft voice, she spoke, "*Shammai*, this tear in the jeans is the latest style. Youngsters love it."

"Style! What style?" *Shammai* said. Kia bit her nails, bowed her head, and stood like a lamb for slaughter. "In my salad days, when I was young and sweet in appearance, I wore sleeveless tops and miniskirts—but never wore such torn clothes," said *Shammai*, reminiscing her past.

With a small face and a wobbly tone, Kia replied, "I know you're absolutely right, but now the culture has changed."

"Enough of your justification! I know this modern way of life only leads to individualistic, independent life." Tongue-tied, Kia twisted her fingers nervously.

Shammai didn't understand this kind of insane style. With a stern voice, she said, "Here's a piece of advice for you. Many moons ago, when I was a young lady, we associated torn clothes only with beggars and destitute people. Our elders encouraged us to stitch up anything that was torn—be it a piece of fabric or a relationship. In relationships, it was painful to forgive, but we never ran away from it." The analogy didn't make sense to Kia, but she could tell that *Shammai* longed to pour out her heart.

Kia said, "I'm sorry, *Shammai*. Please let me go now. If I am not around, my mother will start looking for me."

Shammai took her walking stick, poked Kia's tummy, and sternly said, "No! Give me your ear." She hurled the stick aside, closed her eyes, took a deep breath, and continued, "Once, I tried to mend a relationship between two lovers. It was my fault. I forgot these are modern times, where it's acceptable to leave torn things as they are—just like human relationships. When I went out of my way to reunite them, I was accused of false allegations."

Kia had no idea what *Shammai* was saying. She thought to leave quietly, without her flying disc. She signalled Leader to follow her and took her first step, but *Shammai* caught her wrist, startling her. To her surprise, *Shammai's* mellow face was reflecting a different story, and these words of hers confirmed it. "Yes, they held me responsible for assisting your parents in going away from the family and later for attempting to bring them closer to each other." This piece of information was a bolt from the blue; Kia stood motionless and forgot about her previous decision to go home. *Shammai* faced the kitchen door and said, "Now you may go, I feel much better after sharing a glimpse of truth."

Glancing at her wristwatch, Kia said with a modulated voice, "I think I can spare some minutes."

Shammai continued, "That is the reason your mom must have warned you to stay away from me."

At that very moment, Kia's mind resounded with the words of her mother, Jenny: "Be careful of *Shammai.* She is an awful person who dislikes children, and you should have nothing to do with her."

The twinkling drops of tears in *Shammai's* eyes and the gentle hold of her weak hand persuaded Kia to listen to her story. *Shammai* knew for sure that the non-factual narrative about her by Kia's mother still kept Kia in darkness. Her mother had bent backwards to make sure that Kia didn't feel her dad's absence. While all in her school spoke highly about their fathers, Kia was very keen to know what happened to her dad. Though Kia's mother worked her fingers to the bone to give her a valuable education and to provide expensive dresses, cosmetics, etc., she still longed for a father figure in her life. She missed her daddy, especially when she came home with her friend Nikita and her dad from music classes at around 8pm. As a child, she lost the experience of feeling tall on the shoulders of her daddy, the way her neighbour Joyce did. All the time she played outdoor games with Leader, for she had no tough hands to catch her before she fell. She missed him when she learned to ride a bicycle at nine, while all her friends' dads taught them at a very young age. Whenever she got a refusal from her mother, she had no one else to convince to approve her to buy the things she liked.

Shammai wiped her glasses, and with sparkling eyes and a weightless gaze she said, "It was love that brought them together in marriage."

Leaning over with her hands on her knees, Kia said, "Oh, nice! My parents indeed swam against the current of arranged marriage. Nevertheless, *Shammai,* I don't understand what happened to that love now."

"It's not a short story. If you want to listen to it first, grab something to sit on." Kia rolled an abandoned, seasoned log of a coconut tree and squatted in front of *Shammai.* She rested her charming oval face on her soft, tender palms, which she had never even used to wash her own plate. It was all because of her mother's over protectiveness.

Now she was all eyes and ears, waiting eagerly to hear what *Shammai* had to say about her parents. Before revealing the piece of untold truth, *Shammai* requested her to keep two promises. She said, "Promise me you will not report any part of our conversation to Jenny."

"Why?"

"Because it can lead to a greater misunderstanding, and she will never forgive me."

"I promise, whatever you'll say, I will keep it to myself."

"My heart says that your parents still have love for each other. Now you have to promise me that you will try everything to bring them together."

"How will their reunion help you?"

Shammai, with a smile on her face, said, "I know I will gain nothing, just think how much you will gain." In the back of her mind, she knew she would receive forgiveness and acceptance.

Before deciding upon the second promise, Kia spent a few minutes wondering. To make a serious Kia smile, *Shammai* said, "You are stuck in between like my old 1980s tape recorder."

With a gloomy face and a confused smile, Kia replied, "I am just twelve years old and that too a girl child. What brave act can you expect from a vulnerable child?"

Shammai lifted Kia's chin, hoping her words would chisel through Kia's low self-esteem. "You wisely told me that my stitching this pair of jeans is useless since it comes in the torn form and that is a style, but aren't you aware of the role a young girl can play in today's world?" *Shammai* came closer to Kia and gently placed her hand on her shoulder. "This world has not only changed in the way we dress and the way we eat; it has also changed the way we were and the way we are. In my younger days, it was an impermissible act for a teenager to step out of her house at odd times, especially at night. They literally compelled my only brother to go to school, despite knowing that his interest was only in sports and fishing. Though they sent my sister and me to school, we were never encouraged to pursue higher studies. Society played a major role in those days in a parent's thought process because they understood that a daughter would marry and go away to her husband's house, whereas a son would take care of his parents in their old age."

"But whenever I asked my mother about my daddy, she always told me, 'You are a little girl; what you will understand?' She also stressed that I am a girl child and a man may take advantage of me. This is the fear which has crept into me."

"Yes, I totally agree with your mother, for she spoke from her bitter experiences, and she is not to be blamed for that."

While both *Shammai* and Kia were completely engrossed in their conversation, out of nowhere they found Leader at the nest of a bulbul. He was hounding a tiny, few-weeks-old bird that was battling to fly in the infinite blue sky. Kia promptly rebuked Leader. *Shammai* continued, "We girls should be like that bird. Despite Leader's threat, that baby bulbul did not give up. It flew to the higher branch and not into the nest. In the present world scenario, we shouldn't live in our nest or shell and expect men to provide for us. We need to fly and build our own identity. Nowadays, there is an outstanding transformation in society. We are no longer considered as 'handle with care,' but we can handle almost anything. We can function exceptionally well in all sectors of society. Dear child, don't step back from your accomplishments just because you are a young girl. At least, attempt to do whatever you can do."

Kia said, "*Shammai*, I have a question on my mind."

"You can ask me any of your doubts, for I know both of your parents through and through. I knew your dad as a young bachelor and your mom as a dancer"

Kia asked, "Do you think they still love each other?"

"Yes! I am sure that they still love each other. The fact that both have remained single even now shows that the ember of love is still burning within. They require someone to blow away the ash of misconception and revive the fire of love. And you are the right person to help them forgive and rebuild their relationship with love and trust. Initially, when I spoke to your mom after your dad had left, she was sure that he would come back to her someday. When I asked your dad about dating someone before he lost his years, he told me that he loved only one person in his life and would see no one else."

One more question popped into Kia's juvenile mind: "If they loved each other so much, why did they leave each other?" *Shammai* kept the unmended jeans aside on the wooden arm of her cane armchair. She refilled her tea from the thermos flask, which was kept on the stool next to her, into her empty teacup. She took a sip. Resting back on the chair in a relaxed posture, she said, "I will answer all your questions. First, let me begin the account of your parent's love." Now Kia was all ears to *Shammai*, makes Leader sit down quietly next to her, and eagerly waited for the love story of her parents.

Chapter 3

Seed of Love

Rat-a-tat-tat! I heard. Not on my door, not even on the roof—it was on the floor of the courtyard of my neighbour's magnificent Portuguese colonial house. I stood on my toes and saw a mango seed hitting an empty plant pot. The falling of the seed from nowhere into a well-maintained compound made me inquisitive. "Something is fishy," I said to myself. I dragged a heavy wooden chair from the corner of my veranda and stood on it. The only person I saw was a young and tall man. His hair was covered by ferns that were growing on a rubble fence. He was leaning on the other side of the rough compound wall, his face protruding through the shrubs, which were a little shorter than he was. When he saw me, he ran to the side of a cozy, insignificant house roofed with old semi-cylindrical clay tiles. Its floor was coloured with rough red cement, which wasn't as good when compared to the commonly found polished mosaic of that time. The audacious, debonair man was none other than Toney Lobo, your daddy, Kia.

Right from the beginning, his family was unfortunate; his father's untimely demise was like a bolt from the blue, which led their existence to go from hand to mouth. Toney was the elder of the three siblings—two boys and a girl.

Though it was a colonial house, it had a façade with a rooftop terrace. Its flooring was made of hexagonal ceramic tiles protected by a cardboard false ceiling. This outstanding house in the entire village belonged to your mother, Jenny Gomes. Her family could afford all the comforts of life because her grandfather was a Portuguese government employee when this part of India was a Portuguese colony. That's why her father got the best education, and as a result, locals considered the family to be the cream of society. Jenny was the second among the two princesses of the neighbourhood homes. She was a pretty, bubbly, curly-haired, doe-eyed beauty. Her most attractive feature was the dimple on her chin.

Toney was a smart cookie. Because of his duties on the home front after the demise of his father, he had to discontinue his studies, but he did not want to give up on his future. He pleaded with his mother to permit him to learn to sew from his father's 60-year-old sister—a tailor by profession and ten years older than his dad. That was none other than me, your *Shammai.*

Toney was keen on the tailoring classes. On one occasion, when he enthusiastically came to me to learn to stitch, I asked him about his flawless and well-aimed throw of a chewed, old mango seed, which he had pitched intentionally. He could not hide the fact, for I told him I saw him do it. With all his innocence, without hiding anything, he lifted the veil on their extremely private love story.

Toney, with his solemn, honest face, narrated the very beginning of his love.

****

The love bug bit me at a refreshing spring, appearing out of nowhere amid the green mountains of Solva—a land so serene, adorned with mountains crowned by tropical forests and refreshed by rivers fed by springs gushing from the laterite soil. Jenny had never in her life experienced the grace of the blue sky or been in the reviving mountains inhaling the fresh air. Jenny was born with a silver spoon and was unaware of the world of woods. She always traveled by car or on her father's motorbike. She mostly moved among houses, shops, offices, and other kinds of concrete buildings. Never had she any opportunity to walk amid thorns and thistles or step into the boggy and gritty land.

Jenny and my younger sister Candy were of the same age. They were like two peas in a pod. Most of their interactions in those days revolved around school and church. At fourteen, my sister discontinued her studies, and the only place they would meet thereafter was the church. In all those years, I had no special eye on Jenny—not even a crush on her.

The Spring of Solva was on her bucket list, for she had heard about it from my sister. For Jenny's parents, my sister was her guardian angel. Whenever she would be out of their sight, Candy was the first one to be trusted. After much insistence, her mother sent her with Candy to the spring without her father's knowledge. If my sister Candy was her guardian angel, I was my sister's Archangel Michael. That's the reason they included me in their spring adventure.

It was mid-April, and at noon I was all set and equipped—not externally, but internally—because I had a heavy lunch. From our living room, I could see Jenny, almost half an hour early, equipped with a backpack. She was so excited, and I was sure that she must have had very little food before leaving her house. She was sitting on the fence, balancing the bag and her legs. Her feet were bolted in white and red runners hanging by the side of our compound wall, and a drawstring bag hung on her side towards her home. I didn't know what to do—whether to invite her to the house or plainly tell her to wait there in the scorching one o'clock sun till we were ready to go. Without proceeding further, I took a U-turn, finding myself in the kitchen. It was all because of my shy nature.

On that day, I learned that every woman does not prepare herself in the same manner to go to the same planned destination. For Candy, the destination was as popular as a club. It was clear from the time she spent in front of the mirror. To Jenny, it was a lonely place, but as exciting as watching the sunset at a secluded beach. It was obvious when she basked in the sunlight without hesitation.

Candy then came out with her inexpensive chandelier earrings peeping out from her Panama hat. Our aunt had given her the hat to protect her from tanning while going to school. It was all, which she had to save her from the sun, for we were not fortunate enough to travel by public transportation to school. She was dressed in simple black jeans and a white T-shirt that she had picked up from our late dad's trunk. I saw her outside the house having nothing other than a plastic bag in her hand. I picked my cap, which had a political party symbol right in the center. They gave it free of cost before the state elections. I wore my worn-out rubber flip-flops and carried nothing in my hand. I walked behind them.

On that sunny afternoon, we hit the trail to the spring. The powdered leaves on the path had paved the way. It was about an hour's walk. My sister was leading. I was last and the least to speak. Though trees surrounded us, the path was sun-drenched. I saw Jenny uncovering her coiffed hair, fighting to protect her face from sunburn. I could literally count the times I had spoken to her, and had I said, "Take my hat; it will keep you from suntan," at that moment, it would have been the fourth time I had actually spoken to her. I finally offered her my hat, and she accepted. What do I tell you? I was over the moon. I was constantly looking out for her to keep her safe from thorns and the creeping creatures. I did it because I knew the forest from stem to stern.

On our way, we met with a troop of Gray Langurmonkeys. Their confident strides exhibited their knowledge of the forest. Even some foxes played hide and seek with us, noticing the stone in my hand. The jungle fowl also attempted to visit us, but being shy in nature, they rushed into the bushes.

We proceeded among bushes, shrubs, and trees. These gave us wild fruits and berries as refreshment on our tiresome journey. Jenny was delighted after tasting every new fruit. She was bursting with joy, and she jumped and plucked a berry. It was a sight to behold—her hat falling and her silky hair resting on her tender, naïve face. Her pink capris and her yellow top were sunlit between brown grass and green leaves. All this was imprinted in my mind but had not entered my heart. In her excitement, she even forgot about the thorns which that had pricked her while she was rushing at the sight of ripe *Carissa carandas.*

Jenny was terribly tired from running after every never-seen wild fruit. She got overwhelmed with the jungle—its sharp and soft stones—which were alien to her. Balancing a seasoned bamboo stick on the steep slope, she walked on the uneven ground. A cowman had offered the stick to her, noticing how unstable she was on her feet. She'd rushed to inquire about the welcoming wildflowers. She pointed at the sky when she saw the flight of sparrows and other birds. It was her first outdoor adventure in the woods. Though she was dead tired, her spirit was willing, even on her heavy feet.

The distance covered was more, and now we were just one kilometer away from our destination. Along the way, observing her innocence and non-discriminatory character, I became sentimental. But, the doors of my heart had not yet welcomed her. She was pale with exhaustion. "I think from tomorrow onwards, I should start waking up early in the morning for better stamina," said Jenny.

Candy looked at her from top to bottom and replied, "Yes, you need it." She said that mostly because Jenny was chubby.

"Candy, I would love you to join me at the crack of dawn for a brisk walk, "Jenny said.

Candy answered, "I will think about it."

Pitying my only sister, I said, "Please don't go along. First of all, you look like a stick. If you join her, you'll disappear." Candy was very slim and crazy about maintaining her figure. She furiously picked cashew nuts lying beside the road and hurled them at me. "I will see you later!" she said.

As we were approaching the spring, we could see the water flowing beside us in the form of a rill. It was from the source of the spring. I doubled up to the water and bent to drink. Jenny rebuked me and said, "Please don't drink it. I have clean water."

Candy, in a raucous voice, said, "You don't worry—he even drinks water directly from the pond where he swims."

"No, this is contaminated water. Please take this," Jenny said and walked towards me, holding a water bottle in her hand. Initially, I hesitated and felt ashamed. For just a few minutes before, I had seen her drinking water from that same bottle. She had touched her sweet lips to the crown of the bottle. She guessed what I was thinking and said, "No one will die if we touch our mouth to the bottle." But I was thinking whether I was worthy to touch my lips to the crown. And while I drank the water, I felt as if I was in heaven.

It would take a ten-minute walk to see the refreshing spring. Ahead of us, there was a ten-feet towering crag. Next to it there were inconsequential man-made steps on which a two-year-old child or a seventy-year-old person could walk confidently. But the crag was coated in patches of slippery moss. The lost streams of the spring kept the moss alive. I thought of climbing the crag to create an impression; I kept my feet on a dicey greenish sedimentary rock sculpted by the force of the falling water. I was at the feet of the crag.

"Hey! Please follow us. It's risky to succeed," said Jenny.

"He is not a kid; he understands the danger of climbing on that slimy rock face," replied Candy.

"Yes, I understand, and I am confident," I said.

I was determined to carry on my unnecessary show-off. Although I was anxious as I proceeded higher, to keep up my reputation, I kept ongoing. And when I reached an eight-foot height, the stone well, fed with water, deceived the grip of my fingers. The well-settled moss shook off my worn-out flip-flops. As a result, I plummeted to the same sharply carved sedimentary stone on which I had initially stepped. This mishap lacerated my feet brutally and bruised my knees. Blood oozed like spring.

This was the first dreadful sight Jenny had witnessed in her life. She was dumbfounded. Despite the acute pain and panic I was going through, I said calmly, "Relax, I am ok," only to ease their worries. As soon as Jenny heard my words, she gathered some courage and came down hastily. At the drop of a hat, she fetched her first-aid medicine.

Candy was still half way on those steps at the side of the crag. Noticing Jenny's concern towards me, she told her, "He deserves it. Let him sit here; we'll move on to the spring."

Jenny promptly turned back and said, "I can't leave him here in this pathetic state." By then, she had figured out the depth of my injury. Realizing that there was no sign of a single human inhabitation nearby, the only option that came to her mind was to rush back to the village clinic. As she was applying ointment and bandaging my wound with her handkerchief, she came nearer to me. She looked into my eyes intensely and whispered, "How do you feel now? Do you feel comfortable and nice? Will you be able to walk back?" Oh! That was a moment I will never forget in my life. It had infused her breath of love into my heart. That wounded me within, and only her love for me would be its ointment.

"Come, Jenny, we'll go to the spring and return to him," These words of Candy interrupted the link between us.

Jenny sternly replied, "We can come back some other day to the spring. Right now, the important thing is to see that the bleeding stops. Come, we'll depart." I was so astonished to perceive her sensitivity that I was at a loss for words. Limping and surrendering, I held on to them while descending.

On that day, though we never made it to the spring of Solva, my heart made it to Jenny's heart. Her affectionate gestures towards me turned my perception of her. It is rightly said, 'Don't judge a book by its cover'. I had judged Jenny according to her status and appearance. I had the impression that she was a proud person. No! She was a gem of a person.

My sister was teasing her for bringing along a bag full of unnecessary things. But if you ask me, I would say that she had been well-prepared for any circumstances that came our way. Candy and I had been to the spring many times, but it was Jenny's first time, going through the dense mountains. Even if Jenny's dreams and excitement were shattered, she swallowed it with love. Her benevolent heart captured my being and melted my heart. She had nursed me by falling to her knees in front of me. Who would not fall in love with such an amazing personality?

My injury was a blessing in disguise for Jenny. It became the best excuse for her to visit me at my place. While lying on my couch, if I heard her voice or heard that she was coming, there would be a great chemical reaction in my brain. And beholding her in front of me gave me butterflies in my stomach. That was the sign that I was head over heels for her.

When I was back on my feet, she would look for an opportunity to come over to our place just to talk to me. Her attention had shifted from Candy to me. This reminds me of the time her mother had sent her to our house, saying, "Please go to Candy's house and ask her mother whether they want chikoo plantlets to plant."

Prior to the elections, the government had offered these high-breed grafted chikoo plants freely. Jenny's family had plenty of them because of their father's influence in the government. On that day, Jenny came to our house running. Instead of asking my mother, she rushed to me and asked, "Do you want chikoos?"

I said, "Yes! Why not?" She took full advantage of her stay at our home, and we chit-chatted for a while.

"Jenny! O Jenny! Where are you? Are you there?"Hearing her mother Rosemary's voice, she went back with excitement to return with the chikoos.

As soon as she entered the threshold of her house, she said to her mother, "Mama, yes! They are happy to have some chikoos."

Her mother replied, "What! chikoos? Who told you that I am distributing chikoos?" Jenny was so eager to see me that in her hurry she missed hearing the full sentence. She just heard, "...ask whether they want chikoos." "Plants to cultivate"—that part she missed. By then, she was out of the house. Her mother was very kind. She realised it was her daughter's mistake, so she walked to the dinner hall, grabbed some chikoos from the fruit basket, took a few grafted chikoo plants, and sent them with Jenny to our house. The answer that Jenny gave to cover her mistake amazed me.

She said, "Mama has given these, saying that if you like the taste, you can plant these; they will produce the same variety."

After dispatching the things, she was dawdling when sarcastically Candy commented, "Oh! It's time for lunch." Jenny got the message and left our house. For us, it was Chikoo Day, for we ate and planted on the same day.

Though we had connected at a deeper level, we had not yet expressed our love through letters or in words. I genuinely wanted to know whether she loved me and, if she did, why?

One evening during sunset, Candy and I had taken our cows to graze in the fresh green pasture. Jenny also joined us. The field was full of tender, juicy grass nurtured by early showers. The three of us were resting on the cow's life-size boulder at the corner of the meadow. The cows went on grazing and, without our notice, they entered the bushes beside the grassland. It was Candy's day to look after the cows. She was very concerned about their movement; though her body was beside us, but her soul was with the cows. The sun was on the verge of setting, and it would be difficult to search for them in twilight. So, she left us alone to fetch the cows.

I took advantage of our isolation and asked Jenny, "Do you love me, and if yes, why?"

"Yes, I love you very much," she said.

"You love me despite knowing that I am not well-to-do as your family and not even much educated?" I asked.

She continued, "Yes! I love you as a person. The foremost virtue I like in you is your sensitivity. It's not just because you gave your hat to me on our way to the spring. I remember, a year ago, Candy had lost some money with which she had to purchase a science journal. I found her in a bundle of nerves, crying bitterly in the classroom. She was thinking about how to answer her mother. The following day, she was at ease and content. I asked her the reason, and Candy said, 'My brother Toney is a very sensitive person, and he answered my tears by providing money. He had earned it by painting the window grills at the fabrication workshop. It was the time when he was saving money to purchase fabric to learn to stitch. He put a hold on his passion and offered his hard-earned money to me.' From that day, my feelings grew stronger for you. Now, after being with you for a while and knowing you better, I can't think of anyone other than you."

These flattering words of Jenny evoked such passion in me for her. I descended from the boulder, while she remained seated. With my heart filled with emotions, I stood opposite her. Just behind her, I could see the sun kissing the mountain range and dissolving into its bosom. I, too, kissed Jenny's forehead, rested my head on her arm, and whispered, "I love you too and will always be yours." From then on, we were so deeply in love that we couldn't imagine a world without each other. Our bond of love was obvious to everyone, and as a result, Jenny's parents warned her to stop seeing me.

****

Though Kia was engrossed in her parents' love story, she interrupted *Shammai* and asked, "*Shammai*, did my daddy tell you the reason for throwing the mango seed in my mom's courtyard?"

"Yes!" replied *Shammai* and continued the story.

****

Once all of this happened, they could not meet openly for fear of their parents. Initially, they wrote letters telling each other about their meeting point and delivered them through Candy. However, it was difficult to pass those letters. Jenny's sister, Jane, always monitored her moves. Before Jane could catch Toney and Jenny red-handed, they changed their pattern and began to communicate non-verbally, indicating to each other by pitching a seed in either house's courtyard. Usually, their meeting point was in the forest behind their homes and not in public places. This forest was full of fruit-producing flora like mango trees, cashew trees, kokum trees, jackfruit trees, jamun trees, etc.

The secret behind throwing the mango seed in the courtyard was to indicate they should meet under that tree on that day. They would meet twice a week, if not at least once. This changing of the venue every time would help them stay safe from all suspicions. The day Jenny would find a jackfruit seed in front of her house, she would know that it was a sign to meet Toney under the jackfruit tree. Another thing was that if she discovered a kokum or jamun seed, the hint was not only to meet under those trees, but that there would also be a change in time. Since the kokum and jamun seeds were smaller, at least three to four were easily thrown at a time. This indicated that they had different venues and times for seeing each other. And this completely depended on the seed found in the courtyard. Yes, it is rightly said that lovers are blind, but this couple also kept their families in the shadows.

All this went on for at least four years. Now Jenny was nineteen, and Toney was twenty-three. Being in their parents' clutches, there was no hope of getting married. No one could understand the bond of love between them except Candy and

Toney's mother, Tina, who knew that her son would take good care of Jenny at any cost. He was so sensitive that even if his family member winced, he would ask 'What's wrong? Tell me? Can I do something?'He would sacrifice anything for his loved ones without uttering a single word about his pain. Both were close to marriageable age, but Jenny's family was dead set against Toney's proposal. Things were getting worse. Jenny loved him so much that their class status mattered nothing to her. Though she had never held a needle in her hand, she was willing to help Toney in his work once they were together.

The everyday nagging about Toney and putting him down by her family frustrated Jenny. Jane would take advantage of the situation and also taunt her. The home was like a prison for her; she had everything and yet she had no peace. Even if Jenny helped with the household chores, it was believed that she was doing it to please everyone so that she would be allowed to marry.

Love was not shown to Jenny at all; none of the family members understood her. Instead of helping Jenny to find a solution together, her opinion was neglected. Gomes' family was more concerned about their status than the daughter.

Jenny's family decided to move her to her maternal uncle's place, far from home. Toney and Jenny even contemplated suicide, but Candy helped them get rid of those thoughts."

Shammai breathed deeply and took a break. Next to her was a cup of tea, which was almost lukewarm. She drank it all before it got cold. She stretched her hands and legs for blood circulation. Kia, feeling restless, requested her to continue narrating the story.

Chapter 4

Feliz Navidad

Shammai coughed and smiled at Kia. She stood and asked Kia to move the chair to the shade. This time, Kia was very enthusiastic and happy to listen to her. *Shammai* noticed that Kia showed a great deal of interest in knowing more about her parents. Leaning back, placing a hand on the arm of the chair with a warm voice, *Shammai* continued to tell the story.

****

It was a dense, horrifying, silent, chilly night of the new moon. Jenny walked towards the cemetery and the well of the dead bones. When the mind is blinded by love, the feet don't tremble even a bit to step into the unpredictable darkness on the road.

"Don't admonish me. Love fears nothing that is obscure but fears only the loss of love."That was Jenny's reply to Candy's pleas.

"Please don't go on that strange, abandoned path. It leads to the haunted well behind the graveyard. It contains bones and choked springs."

Candy, a person known for getting scared of her own shadow, had no guts to follow Jenny. Moreover, there was no moonlight, and she had heard about how late Peter's doppelganger was sighted in the dark night at the graveyard. Candy did not dare to lift her leg in that direction. She came hastily to me, trembling with fear and tears in her eyes.

She said, "Auntie Maria! Jenny has moved further, away from the streetlights, and has gone into the darkness of the cemetery. She has now reached behind the cemetery and has turned towards the well." Presuming that Jenny would jump in the well, which was filled with bones from the graves that were emptied for the corpse, Candy whimpered and continued, "The other day, I spoke to her about freedom in life. But I didn't tell her to give up on her life. I just said that instead of giving up your life, just run away from this suffocation and live somewhere freely."

Wasting no time, I said, "Right now, please keep calm and don't worry. She is safe. And I plead with you not to speak about it to anyone, not even to your mother. It will be a great favour for the sake of your boon companion's freedom." I was confident because I played a crucial role in Toney and Jenny's arrangements. I also had absolute trust in Candy, for she was someone who would take a secret to the grave. For instance, Candy knew Toney and Jenny's meeting points.

"*Shammai*, will you please hold on! Can you tell me in what way you were involved in the plan and what was the plan? Was it to commit suicide? If so, who saved them?"

"Kia, my darling, yes, they informed me about their plan. But what you think is not correct. Before you misunderstand, let me throw some light on your misconception.

"It was at the end of the calendar year 1984 and in the middle of December. I left my house on one chilly morning to go to the village church. After the mass, followed by the national flag hoisting on the occasion of the state's Liberation Day, I walked back home. Unlike other days, I reached home by brunch, and on my arrival, I heard loud music in the homes of my neighbours, who couldn't see each other face to face. Among them, one neighbour was vibrating the wall of his house by playing "Feliz Navidad" (3)

Prospero año y felicidad (Merry Christmas, a prosperous year and happiness), which is a Christmas carol. The other neighbour was blasting his house with the song *Mere Desh ki Dharti* (the land of my country), a patriotic song from a Bollywood movie. The melody from both sides was making an ear-splitting sound. It was no more music but just noise. It was like a tug of war between two hate-filled neighbours. In the heat of passion, they thought a louder volume would be the winner.

That significant day was the 19th of December. The day is marked as the Liberation Day of Goa. After the Independence of India in 1961, they overthrew the Portuguese rule in Goa with the support of the Indian army. Later, Goa became a part of the Republic of India. This was the reason why they were playing patriotic songs and Christmas carols. With all this annoyance, I too got disturbed. I was having a tug of war within me. Though I had planned a lot mentally that day, still my thoughts got stuck in various shades of gray. I had to look back on my intentions and make sure that my decision was right. The plan was ethically wrong, but at the heart level, it was genuine. I discovered the answer to my uncertainty in the tug of war between the patriotic song and the Christmas carol. I realized that it was the day to sing patriotic songs. Since we celebrate Liberation Day once a year, the entire day should be dedicated to it. We can play Christmas carols the entire advent season. Similarly, one night would be a life-changing night for Toney and Jenny. Otherwise they would suffer all the days of their lives.

Then, I had some peace of mind. I willingly wanted to assist them in the completion of their plan. I proceeded cautiously towards my neighbour's home and told them that they had the entire season to play the Christmas carols. This is the only day to play patriotic songs. The rest of the days of the year will not bring in the same excitement and delight. Giving them my piece of advice, I lifted my jute bag by the straps and placed it on my shoulders. Without waiting for their response, I continued walking in the direction of the bus stop and boarded a bus to a place called Seachol.

Seachol is an island. During those days, there was no chance of reaching there without a ferry, and it was difficult for the common folk to commute to the city. As a result, it was a scarcely occupied place. Seachol is like a patch of a fresh green mountain, planted in the middle of a broad river. Nature adorned it with emerald, lush vegetation and a blusher of fertile soil. It was the place to find music in nature's conversation with the crickets and katydids chirping, rattling, and humming at night and the tweet chirp sound made by birds in the morning. The constant accompaniment of the resonance of the flowing water and the rustling of the leaves with the breeze was the foundation for all the various sounds. All this composed a melody never heard before and could never be produced. This place, which was enveloped with silence, was my husband's native place. Predominantly, it was the place occupied by the native Hindus of Goa. In his ancestral house, his brother's family once lived, but later, they shifted to Bombay. This out-of-the-way place and that too with a vacant house, would serve as the best location for our plan.

The bus ride was not so pleasant. I stood for almost half of my journey. To remain standing on the jam-packed bus on bumpy roads is like being in a washing machine. The only difference is that instead of being washed and rinsed, you come out with other people's dirt and your sweat. Since I had to get off at the last stop, I decided to sit on the bus for a while. Thankfully, I made it on time, just before the ferry could leave. It was noon when I disembarked the ferry. I stepped on the moist land surrounded by mangrove. I walked for about six minutes and arrived at my husband's ancestral residence. The house was in excellent condition from the outside, but the gardens surrounding the house had gone to the dogs, for no one was around to water and do the weeding. I opened the compound gate and unlocked the door. The creaking sound of the door proved that the house had not been in use for months. All the things in the house were in their proper place, as the owners had arranged them after their annual holiday. It was not dirty, but dusty, as a layer of dust settled like a creeper from the floor to the furniture and to the wall clock till the ceiling fan. I had to spend the rest of my day cleaning the house. On my way, I bought some fresh vegetables from the vendors at the jetty. I switched on the refrigerator and placed it along with bread, butter and milk. By the time I changed the dusty window curtains and replaced the bed sheets, it was 4:30pm, my usual time for tea. I took out the packet of tea from my jute bag and prepared some plain black tea. With that, I was sure that the cooking stove was working, and the refrigerator was running. To deceive the passers-by and deflect thieves, I left the house lights switched on.

While returning home, I could choose the best place to sit on the bus, for it was the starting point of the trip. Since Christmas was around the corner, so my journey back home was illuminated by Christmas lights. After a long day's work, the beautiful decorations, embellished trees, and houses invigorated me. After reaching home exhausted , I hit the sack early. Although my early-morning dreams were daunting, filled with people running helter-skelter, I can still say I slept soundly that night.

The next morning, Jenny visited me with her old, torn clothing; some to alter and the others to stitch. Jenny could take nothing out of the house without prior permission. Since her bond with Toney was very obvious to everyone, she was being followed. Jenny's sister Jane was a notorious complaint box. If there was anything fishy, she would complain immediately to her parents. So Jenny had to be extra careful with her activities. Just to avoid her sister, who followed her like a tail, she lied to her parents, saying that she was taking her clothes to my place to have them altered. Her parents agreed to let her go, since I was the only tailor living nearby. The intention was to pack the same clothes and have them sent to the house in Seachol. To make planning easy, I had to tell my husband about our plan, although he already suspected my actions. We loved each other so much that nothing could be kept a secret between us.

My husband had a motorbike, and I felt it would be easy to transport the bag of clothes with him to his ancestral house in Seachol. I had received both Toney's and Jenny's essential clothing to be dispatched. To make my husband's journey comfortable on the bike, I thought of packing their outfits together in a big backpack, which would be convenient to carry on the two-wheeler. As I was rearranging Jenny's clothes, to my amazement, I discovered a bundle of money in the pocket of her suit trousers. It was a sum of ten thousand rupees, and in those days it was an enormous amount. I also found gold ornaments consisting of a necklace, chains, bangles, and earrings, which were rolled in another dress. It stunned me to see the gold ornaments, and I was a bit taken aback because it was a question of gold and money. What I had promised to lend to them was peanuts compared to what she had in her bag. Neither did I have the slightest idea of including this possession in the initial plan, nor was I informed about it. For a while, I felt that to be a part of their plan was like biting the bullet. That night, I couldn't dream or sleep. I could only keep vigil, contemplating what would result from the plan.

"Oh! *Shammai*, you are going on and on, saying plan-plan. Will you please tell me what the plan was?" Kai said with a heavy sigh. *Shammai* grinned from ear to ear and, with a calm voice, carried on the narration.

My dear Kia, this plan was executed at midnight, on the day when Christ was born. Amidst the chilly night vigil, illuminated with miniatures and running lights, carols resounded all around. Toney and Jenny had planned to flee. From the 24th morning till Christmas Eve, both didn't show any signs of escaping to anyone.

It was the moment of the Christmas wave reaching almost to the point of culmination, which engaged all the flock to move their hands and feet to give the last touches. Even Jenny remained busy till noon, decorating the house and keeping it neat. From afternoon onwards, she spent her time in painting her nails and ironing her mother's and her own clothes for the midnight mass. Later in the evening, after a shower, she dressed for the midnight mass. She spent 30 minutes drying and tying her hair in a French braid. For another 30 minutes, she was engaged in applying make-up and getting herself ready; she looked like a celestial being. Throughout the day, she remained as calm as a cucumber.

Toney too was busy. In the morning, he got occupied with completing the unfinished shirts and trousers of the customers who needed them for Christmas. From the afternoon onwards, Toney extended his helping hand to his brother, who was busy giving the finishing touch to the Christmas crib outside in the courtyard. His last work of the day was to hang up the star which he had made from tender bamboo. He covered the star with a white cloth for better visibility at night, hooked it to the outer branch of the guava tree, and made sure that the bulb was lit inside. He pretended to be very normal. No one would believe what was being cooked in his mind.

This was the night which would make a great impact on Toney and Jenny's lives. It was the night they would always remember: a night of their redemption, a night also marked as the birth of the redeemer of the world. This couple in love took advantage of the dense night. Throughout the day, they showed no sign of their decision. The hour to implement the plan into action was approaching soon, and they were losing control of themselves.

Their behaviour, amalgamated with mixed emotions, was obvious at the church during the midnight mass. The omission of the prayers and performing the sacred signs and gestures incorrectly at the Holy Eucharist were clear-cut signs of being physically present but mentally absent. Immediately after the solemn Christmas midnight service, they planned to meet. The meeting point was behind the cemetery, next to the well full of human bones. The graveyard was a quarter of a kilometre away from the church. Since it was not next to the main road, naturally, it escaped the street lights.

Kia! Do you remember these words now? 'Please don't go on that strange, abandoned path. It leads to the haunted, profound well which is at the back of the graveyard. It is a well with dead bones and choked springs.' These were Candy's words on that new moon night, requesting Jenny not to proceed. And this was the statement which I had already mentioned in the beginning, and these are the moments which I would like you to know. These are the very words of your mother, who reported the whole incident to me when I visited her in Seachol.

Kia crossed her legs, rested her chin on her palm, and her elbow on her thigh. Without interrupting, she keenly listened and was excited to know what her mother Jenny had to say.

Shammai wiped her nose with her wrist and continued, "Let me share with you, in Jenny's own words, what happened on that memorable Christmas night."

****

"I've never had such a courage- and emotion-filled experience in my life. That night, I realized that to be lost in the congested city is better than being lost in one's own bundle of thoughts. In the city, you have strangers around to ask for directions. In the baffled state of mind, there is no one to listen, and I couldn't dare to ask directions for the not-so-pleasing decisions of my life. Though I was coming back home with the congregation, I could not share my state of mind with anyone. It was like feeling lonely in a crowded railway station.

On that night, I was with Candy and didn't go with my parents in their vehicle after the mass. To keep it insusceptible, I informed my parents that I would return with my friends. However, I was cautious enough not to give out their names; I just mentioned some common names of my friends. While we were walking back home, my eyes were hunting for my beloved. I thought he must be already waiting for me at the proposed place. I couldn't waste a single minute without seeing him. I was ready to escape the group. When we approached closer to the cemetery, I lingered behind. Candy noticed that I went towards the cemetery. Murdering the fear of lost souls, I marched sternly towards the well and the wall of the cemetery. Candy tried to prevent me. After noticing my adamant behaviour, I saw her running towards the elders.

As soon as I reached behind the cemetery, I called out to Toney. I heard no response. I got scared, for I was beside the dead in dead silence. The firefly's light was the only light that kept my heart warm before it could turn cold. The extended rattling trill sounds of the cicada were like the only words of comfort to me in the deadly stillness. In the biting cold, I sat down, folding my legs and knees, facing the darkness. I gently pulled the woollen shawl over my shoulder. I brought it over my head like a caterpillar in a cocoon.

'Jenny, Jenny are you there?' This call from Toney took away all the fear, and I stood up in excitement. As a butterfly would spontaneously kiss the flower for nectar, I kissed him on the cheek and hugged him for warmth. With tears in my eyes, I let him know that I was all alone for 15 minutes. 'Oh, my love! From now on, I will never leave you alone,' he whispered. Holding tight to my shoulders with his silvery voice, he said, 'I didn't want to make it obvious to my friends that I was in a hurry. All of them stayed back after mass to play the annual Christmas Housie. So, I bought a ticket to play. Once it started, all ears were on the next number, and in that silence I took the French leave.' That was the reason he gave for his delay.

I said, 'Never mind, what's next?'

He replied, 'We will have to walk for a while through the fields. He seemed uncertain, wearing a sky-blue shirt with a loose maroon tie and rolled sleeves, which hinted at his nervousness. He extended his right hand and held my shoulders tightly and walked. I walked along with him to my freedom, but what a paradox it was. I had to cover my face with the shawl while I was marching towards my freedom.

That Christmas night, with festivity all-around, whoever was seen around was quite tipsy. At the corner of my eye, I saw a young man in the dim streetlights. He wore shorts and a red collarless T-shirt. The color suited the season, but the attire did not. It was that night; Toney introduced me to Raju for the first time. He was the fifth person who knew about our plan. Raju was Hindu, and that kept him available and out of the Christmas celebrations that night. Raju and Toney were best friends. They were employees of the same tailoring shop called The Fashion Touch. Raju had parked his motorbike in the dark. Offering the keys and lending his helmet, he pointed at his Hero Honda Splendour. Now I realized why Toney was anxious: he doubted Raju's lazy nature, but not his ability to keep secrets.

We mounted the motorbike; I held him tight, and we hit the road to Seachol. After four kilometers, the traffic police halted us. A doubt arose in my mind that a hunt for us may have started, for my father was influential in the government. Like an obedient youth, Toney slowed down the bike. He turned back, keeping his helmet on. He could only see my eyes. Looking into it, he whispered not to uncover my face. He had no clue about the documents of the bike. He pretended to open the pouch, which was fixed on the petrol tank of the bike.

The officer turned to us. For a moment, my heart was in my mouth, and I could feel Toney's heart beating very fast. The officer approached us. He deliberately ignored Toney's fear-filled fake smile. With a grumpy face, he straight away brought the breathalyzer closer to his mouth. Realizing that Toney was alcohol-free, the officer said, 'Nights like Christmas are prone to drink-and-drive mishaps, so we are keen to check if there is any alcohol content in the body. Now you can go.'

Then I let my hair down and thanked God. I leaned on Toney with a long sigh, resting my head on his back. Breaking through the chilly wind, we continued our journey. While I was traveling on the motorbike, floating in the breeze with closed eyes and arms embracing Toney, a thought popped into my mind: today is Christmas Day, a day of kisses and gifts. Would I be able to compensate for those hugs with one person and not share any gifts? Spontaneously, a pacifying thought arose in my mind: It's fine this year, next year, we will all be together with our families. Once we get married, our families will have no other option than to accept our union.

Meanwhile, the breeze turned into freezing cold, and I figured out that we were approaching closer to the river which we had to cross to get to our destination. Early in the morning, at around 4 o'clock, we reached the jetty and spent an hour waiting for the first ferry at 5 o'clock to go to Seachol. Yes, it's right! Time flies, and especially when you're with your loved one, that one hour passed quickly, as if it was just a few seconds."

****

"Kia, this is what your mother told me about their escape to Seachol."

"*Shammai*! Why did they go to Seachol?" Kia asked. *Shammai*, straightening her back and stretching her shoulders, continued the story.

"Do you remember? I had told you about my husband's family house in Seachol. That was their destination. Once they reached Seachol, they headed to that house to stay unidentified till they could get married. When they made it to the house, they were at ease in the cozy house.

When Toney and Jenny were fulfilling their dreams, the village of Raia was in hot water. Raia was a place with lots of houses. They could hear every whistle of the pressure cooker in the next house, and the aroma of *chorisam* (sausages) would travel to another house without delay. Therefore, the message about Jenny missing spread quickly. There was great chaos and commotion in the entire village.

The phone line of Jenny's house was busy calling friends and relatives. The doorbells of the neighbours rang early in the morning, and Jenny's father, with the help of the police was searching for Jenny. Except for Toney's house, they searched every house; just because they were not on good terms, they skipped it. At first, they thought that someone had kidnapped her. So initially, they had no clue that she had eloped. Jenny's father even made himself responsible for her abduction. He held a powerful post in the government and would not go against his conscience at any cost. As a result, he made many rivals who were waiting to discover his weak points. Jenny was his weakness, for she was the combination of beauty and intelligence. He would also share Jenny's achievements proudly with others. This led him to conclude that it was the work of his adversaries. But what was most surprising was that there was no call from the kidnappers till 6 in the morning. He tried his best to gather information through his friends about any suspicious activities detected at the location of his foes. The report he got was that all was calm.

Toney's family was tension-free and did not know what was happening in the vicinity. They thought he had gone with his friends for a Christmas party and would come back around 6:00 in the morning. It was around 6:30am when Toney's mother, Tina, got up to start her cooking for the festive day. With half-sleepy eyes, as she was passing his room, she was shocked to notice Toney's bed empty. All her drowsiness went away instantaneously. She also learned that there was no news from Toney explaining his delay. Tina alarmed her daughter, Candy, and her younger son, Jack, by deliberately pouring a mug of water. Once both were actively listening, Tina told them that Toney was missing. Now there was no time to lose. They freshened up and went out, inquiring about his absence. What they heard was that Jenny was also missing from her home. When the public got to know that even Toney was missing, the news of their escape spread like wildfire in the village. Toney's family was in total darkness and puzzled about what was happening around.

Jenny's father threatened and blamed Toney's family for being a part of their plan. When Toney's family learned of the accusation against them, they were speechless and helpless.

Toney's mother, Tina, was a simple, industrious woman. She toiled day and night as a housemaid to bring up her children. She was not as influential as Jenny's father was, so she could not withstand the allegations. With sincerity on her face and tears in her eyes, she reported to the police that she had no clue about their escape. She begged the officer not to harm her son if they found him. Within two days, the families had inquired with every affiliated person and searched all over, but hadn't found a single hint. Those of us who knew about their arrangements kept it a secret. The police officer, after understanding that their search had gone in vain, commented, "During the Christmas season, we celebrate the feast of Epiphany. The significance of this feast is to pay homage to the three kings from a distant land who had come to the newly born universal king. They had the star as the sign which led them to the birthplace of Jesus. With Toney and Jenny, it is tough to trace because they left no sign for their families, nor did we find any clue about where they settled after their flight. The only thing we can do is wait and watch for their return. If they come back after marrying, they will be beyond our limits to be accused and arrested, for both of them are of the legal age of marrying."

Mr. Gomes, raising his eyebrow, said, "Jenny is 19.She is not mature; she is my little girl. He is the one who is responsible; he is 23."

"For you she is young, but in the sight of the law, she has reached the legal age of marriage," said the police officer.

As days, weeks, and months passed by, the situation subsided. The Lobo family accepted the fact that Toney had committed a blunder, and they could do nothing. The Gomes family could not digest the truth that Jenny would commit such an act, ruining the family's name and reputation. Even if she begged for forgiveness, they would not forgive her, as in their eyes, she didn't deserve it.

Chapter 5

Baby's Magic

My dear Mama!

Greetings from your prodigal daughter, Jenny. I hope Papa, Jane, and you are in the pink of health. I understand the agonizing phase you must have undergone after I fled with Toney. Since then, I have received no reply to the first letter I wrote to you. Mama, although the memories of me may have faded from your mind, they remain dear to me, and I will treasure them till my last breath. I know I have failed you as an obedient daughter, but you've always been a mother par excellence, and I'm sure you have a little residue of love left for me in your broken heart.

You know, Mama, I now understand your worth. I miss you, especially when I try something new while cooking. The recipe books in my kitchen keep multiplying, but they add no taste to the food I cook, as love was the essential ingredient you used to include in your recipes. I am sure every nook and cranny of our enormous house was familiar with you, for you said hello to every article in our house every morning while cleaning and mopping. You were like an unpaid housekeeper, making everyone comfortable without uttering a single word. Here, I stay in a one-BHK flat, and it is tedious to keep it clean and nice. Mama, do you know what I do when I go shopping? I buy vegetables that look good on the outside but turn out to be rotten inside when I chop them. I remember the times you bought vegetables from the street hawkers and vendors, always selecting the good ones. But you never bargained with them, for you knew very well they earned so little and had families to be taken care of.

I'm extremely sorry for stealing the money and the gold, but I'm not at all sorry for taking yours and Papa's photograph with me. It helps me to overcome my weaknesses when I look at it. You know of my irrational fear of creepy creatures like cockroaches and lizards. We could barely find them at our house, and even if we did, you would either chase or spray insecticide on them before I could even notice. Here, I find them here every fortnight, and the first word I utter when I notice them is 'Mama'. That is the time I grab your photo and talk to myself, asking, 'What should I do?' I hear nothing, but it reminds me of your words 'Don't worry darling. I am with you, chase it with the broom.' Mama, I reminisce every knock you gave me on my head. It wasn't because I didn't study. It was for my distraction while I sat, combing and eliminating the nits and lice from my head. Here, there is no one to comb my hair. Mama, these are the few memories that I still cherish. If I had to write everything you did for me out of your love, no words would be sufficient.

Mama, I'm not writing all this because I want you to get emotional and change your mind about accepting me. I am writing this letter to inform Papa and you that you both are now grandparents. I know I cannot dissolve the bitterness you have against me, but I hope and wish that my baby girl's face will bring a sweet smile to your face. Mama, my little angel reminds me of your fondness for babies and children. When I caress my baby, it reminds me of the tender love you showed to my little sister Jane when she was an infant. When Jane was too young to speak, you would immediately guess her needs. If Jane cried out of hunger, you would instantly know that she needed to be fed. If she felt under the weather and cried bitterly, you would understand she wasn't keeping well. I also recollect memories of me, especially when I didn't win in competitions. Your consoling words would be 'you haven't lost, you have taken one more step towards greater victory." I always thank God for blessing me with a mother like you.

Mama, you know my baby's face resembles yours. When her tiny, fragile fingers search for a clasp, I wish she held your hand first. When she crawls with her adorable feet, I wish she would crawl straight into your arms. When her pretty, flawless eyes droop with sleep, I wish she would fall into a profound slumber on your bosom. When she smiles, I wish she would chase away your anxieties. When she gets agitated and bursts into tears, I wish she were comforted on your shoulders. When her hair grows a few inches long, I wish she would leap onto your lap so you could comb it and style it the way you did for me and Jane. You are free to ignore my wishes, Mama, but I'll be overjoyed if my daughter's wish to call you 'grandma' comes true. We haven't baptized her yet, and we will wait patiently for your reply with a name for our newborn baby. My last prayer is not for my acceptance but for my innocent daughter to be welcomed into her large family. I believe that you hold the remote to Papa's temper and the keys to the door of his heart. I hope you will use them to convince him. Please convey my regards and love to Papa and Jane.

Love you,

Jenny.

Kia scratched her head with a small voice and said, "*Shammai*, if this was my mother's second letter to her mama, and you helped her to write it, then when did she write the first letter, and how long did they live in Seachol?" *Shammai* paused for a while, raised her eyebrows, and continued speaking.

"Yes! I assisted her in writing this second letter considering the situation at her parents' place. Let me tell you what happened in Seachol, and you will have all your questions answered."

****

The first time I visited them in Seachol, it was their wedding day, and both were in seventh heaven. There was no doubt that God had made them for each other. Toney and Jenny believed that time heals, and they were confident that after they exchanged their nuptial vows, their families would accept them. Their parents were religious and would not separate what God had united. Hence, immediately after their marriage, Jenny wrote her first letter while they lived in Seachol. In fact, both Toney and Jenny wrote letters to their families to inform them of their marriage. The intention behind the letters was to plead for forgiveness and acceptance. Toney received a reply from his mother, starting with a lecture for being insensitive and ending with a note of acceptance. Jenny, however, waited for a reply from her family, but there was no response for months.

They longed to be a part of their family, not because they were unhappy or sad, but because they missed them. As a newly wedded couple, they were having a whale of a time in each other's company. They had converted the vacant ancestral house into their love-nest. To me, they looked like a very *lovey-dovey* couple, whispering sweet nothings while looking into each other's eyes. I observed these acts of love and more when I stayed with them for a while.

At times, I wondered whether it was a blessing or a burden to say 'Yes' to every appeal made in love. I found it hard to judge them for marrying for love because love just happens. It melts and moulds the lovers into oneness, remaining always a mystery. In their married life, 'Yes' was always the answer to each other's requests, leaving no space to express the hardships they would undergo by saying 'Yes'. I remember one occasion when I was on a break and staying with them. One day, when Jenny said 'Yes,' she had to pay a price for it.

Toney had a great hobby of cultivating vegetables in his leisure time. God had blessed Seachol with fertile land, and having ample space around the house was like a cherry on the cake. Toney used the most of the property. Behind the house, beside a cluster of banana trees, there was an empty plot exposed to the sunlight. He cleared and tilled that ground. With love and patience, he sowed a variety of vegetable seeds. It was the early monsoon season, and most of the seeds quickly germinated. On one cloudy morning, as the garden turned green with tiny saplings, it rained cats and dogs all day and night. The rains caused destruction. The furrows flooded with rainwater. The saplings, with shallow roots level, floated away, while others drowned. The ones with deeper roots were tall enough to withstand the disaster. Something had to be done before the situation worsened.

Early in the morning, when Toney discovered the damage, he dropped to his knees, hitting his head. His commitment to his job would not allow him to take time off. The ferryboat's schedule would not spare him if he left late for work, and these irregularities were not acceptable for a new employee. Meanwhile, at home, the vegetable garden was in a terrible state. It was his baby, and it had to be saved before it was ruined. In this tight situation, the only person he could rely on was his wife, Jenny. As Toney rushed to work, he requested Jenny to dig a deep trench around the garden to let the water to drain out. Though digging and scraping wasn't her cup of tea, without hesitation, she said 'Yes' for the sake of love. However, beholding the toil in the paddy field is not equivalent to holding a pickaxe and spade. Jenny had never worked the cultivating land before. Her parents had always taken care of her like a flower, never letting her grow plants in her own life.

For the first time, she stepped into the vegetable garden. With her legs sinking into the soggy mud and holding the drenched spade, she pitched herself into the task. It took her hours to complete what Toney could have finished in an hour. She was exhausted that day, and although she was in physical agony, she smiled through it. She said 'Yes' and endured all this trouble because of her love for him. In the silence of my mind, a thought emerged: Does loving someone mean making sacrifices without expressing the hardship? Or is love about going deep, like a root, to truly understand your loved one? Another thought came to my mind about the seedlings with shallow roots. They always hope to go deeper. Similarly, as Toney and Jenny persevered in their married life, they grew strongly rooted in each other's love day by day.

On the whole, Toney and Jenny were a happily married couple in Seachol. It was their second-to-none place. Jenny became pregnant just a few months after their marriage. Jenny's labor came two days early, and that evening, Toney hadn't yet returned from work. Every passing minute amplified her pain and fear. In her excruciating condition, she could not leave the bedroom. By the time Toney arrived, Jenny was on the floor, weeping in agony. He was so nervous that he could not think clearly. He screamed and called for help. Immediately, the neighbours arrived, and they rushed her to the quay to be taken to the city hospital. However, the ferry had already sailed to the other side of the river. The ferry schedule was strict. After 6pm, only one ferry boat operated until 11pm. Using the emergency procedure, they left the headlights of the Kondolker's Maruti van—in which Jenny was lying—on, and the motorbikes beside them also kept their headlights on.

The ferry boat operators showed remarkable sagacity in recognizing the urgency and quickly returned. Meanwhile, Toney, unable to see Jenny in such agony, tried his best to calm her.

The sight of Jenny's pain compelled everyone nearby to gather. They surrounded the van, where Jenny was sobbing in agony. They offered various suggestions: one said, 'let her out for fresh air,' another reassured them that the hospital was nearby, while someone recommended them to not wait for an ambulance. Suddenly, Jenny collapsed. All the suggestions fell silent as Jenny lost consciousness. For a while, everyone stood, jaws dropped.

When the ferry arrived, everyone was silent. The situation was out of control and people present there joined their hands in prayer. On the other side of the shore, everything was quiet—no ambulance, no traffic, no streetlights on the highway—but soon, they found themselves at the city hospital. As soon as they reached, they rushed Jenny to the operation theatre. After examining her condition, the doctors delivered heartbreaking news to Toney: the situation was critical, and they could save only one life. They asked him who he would want to save. Toney's heart sank when he heard the news. With a heavy heart, he replied, "I haven't seen my child yet, but I've known and lived with my wife. I would want to save my Jenny." They immediately handed him a consent form to sign. After the formalities, Jenny underwent surgery. A neighbour consoled Toney, saying, "I thought both of them had passed away. Thank God Jenny's life is safe."

Jenny remained unconscious throughout and had no recollection of the past few hours. When she came to her senses, she longed to see her child, but there was no baby beside her. Toney was in a miserable condition and could not bear to convey the sad news. By then, I was already at the hospital. In a feeble voice, Toney requested me to speak to Jenny. When I entered Jenny's room, she said to me, "Aunt Maria, they have taken my baby away. I don't know where they have taken her."

Her words reminded me of Mary Magdalene from the Bible. When Mary Magdalene arrived at Jesus' tomb, she saw two angels and said to them, "They have taken my Lord away, and I don't know where they have put Him." At that moment, Jesus appeared to her and revealed that He was not dead, but alive. With this gospel passage in my mind, I spontaneously replied, "Your baby is in heaven with Jesus." With those words, Jenny understood that her baby was no more. She was stunned, her heart filled with grief, and her eyes filled with tears. From then onwards, this painful experience haunted Jenny throughout her stay in Seachol, as both she and Toney blamed the geographical location of Seachol for taking their infant's life.

To overcome the trauma, Toney and Jenny moved to Panjim city and rented a flat in a housing complex named Babu, right in the heart of the city. Panjim was a concrete jungle, with little open land. The air quality was poor, but the quality of life was better. In this busy city, Panjim, the garbage bins were full and stinking, but there were also empty posts creating job opportunities. So, Toney looked for a better job. In this modern city, while the disturbance and noise of vehicles persisted day and night, there was peace and thoughtfulness, among the immediate neighbours. Here, Toney and Jenny had everything at hand.

Though Toney's travel fare was saved, they were now paying rent, and his salary mostly went towards it. House expenditure also went up, because life in the city was as cheap as they had expected. The flat was small, but their hearts were big enough to accommodate anyone. The house would often be packed with neighbourhood children, keeping Jenny occupied. She welcomed all the children to play in their house and gave lessons free of cost to primary students who couldn't afford to pay her. Making ends meet in the city was a laborious task for Toney. Setting aside the entire expenditure, by the end of the month, he would save nothing. Sometimes, he even incurred debt. Without complaining, and occasionally borrowing money from others, he would manage to run the house. He never mentioned the hardships he was going through to Jenny. He always wished that Jenny would charge the students for tuition. Not the entire amount, but at least the minimum fee. That considerable amount would definitely cover the bills of her quarterly beauty parlour visits and her outfits for every festive occasion.

It was love that kept them blind to the sacrifices both of them were making for each other. Their married life revolved around the word 'Yes'. Three years went by, but they never said 'No' to each other. Jenny was expecting a child for the second time. On December 19th, she delivered a baby girl. And that baby was you, Kia. You were six months old when your mom wrote her second letter to her mama. And this time, within two weeks, your mom received a reply to her letter. I was glad when Jenny gave it to me to read.

My dear lost angel Jenny,

Greetings from your mama. I received your letter, and we are all in good health, by the grace of the Almighty. I hope you find this letter in good health as well. I believe Toney loves you and takes care of you. I pray that your married life brings upon you the choicest blessings. My beloved, when you went missing, we were deeply disturbed. We didn't even know what to do and where to search. Your papa searched for you like a mad dog, here, there, and everywhere in and around the village. He woke up all your friends and enemies that night. He did all this because he loved you, and you know that very well. Do you remember when you were found missing at the annual fair when you were eight years old? Papa didn't even go to the organizers to announce; he just yelled, "I am missing my daughter, has anyone seen her?" He was like a small boy screaming amidst the crowd to buy the toys at the church fare.

Because of your absence, he remained gloomy for almost a week. Jenny, you know, when you were not with us, we not only missed you but also your generosity. In your absence, papa even said "Jenny please get my tea," because you were the one who gave it to him without fail every day after work. If your papa needed anything or any help, he would call out to you first. It was only because he was sure that you would never say no to him. Though you were fashionable and spent money lavishly on yourself, yet you were caring and would never say no to anyone for anything. We have not forgotten you, child. But your behaviour hurt us. Sometimes, we think, what was it that we lacked in our parental love, which failed to keep you happy?

When I received your first letter, we could not forgive you. By then, you were both married, and we couldn't take any action against you. Papa had nothing to say after reading your first letter. He always wished you would repent and return without marrying. The very next moment, he tore the letter and threw it in the garbage. He got upset because he was expecting your phone call or a telegram immediately after you moved from the house, to confirm that you were safe. Yes, it was quite tough for us to reconcile with you. It was really difficult for your papa and for me to pardon you. Yes, it hurts to forgive, but the result is reconciliation and the restoration of the relationship. If the pricking of the needle stitches the cloth, then I thought, why not forgive you and restore our bond? Yes, there is gain after every pain. Your sister Jane was not in favour of accepting you back. It's all because, after you ran away from the house, her life here at home became stricter. Her freedom was curtailed, and her visits were restricted only to relatives and old friends.

Imagining the delightful face of our grandchild, our hearts melted. Your baby's magic also worked on your papa, and he is eagerly waiting to see the little angel. Though forgiving was painful, the baby was like a balm to the agitation after the reconciliation. We are now longing to see our grandchild. We will fulfill your wish of naming the baby. Papa has suggested the name Kia, and I hope you will like it. You need not worry about the dress and the expenditure for the christening our grandchild. I have even started my old hobby of knitting wool in Crosia, and I plan to weave sweaters, socks, and beanie hats for my little princess. I am so excited to see her in matching woollen colors. It will thrill me to hear her blabbering while pulling my hair and nose. Papa has also left the doors open for you to stay at our place. You are also free to settle at Toney's house. I am longing to see and embrace you back, my dear Jenny. With these few words, I end my letter.

"*Shammai*, now I know how my parents united with their family. But I don't understand what happened to Aunt Jane after that?" *Shammai* changed her sitting position and continued.

"Well! When all that happened, all attention shifted to Jane. Initially, she loved it. But when it was time to choose a life partner, she had no say. The boys who had a crush on her looked at her, but she always feared displaying any positive signs.

Years passed after Jenny's escape. It was 7 pm, and after shutting the doors and windows, mosquitoes had no chance to come into the house to distract you while praying and sleeping. The silence deepened when the lights were on in the house. The aroma and the utensils had just settled in the kitchen. The Gomes family was waiting to have dinner before it became lukewarm. It was past 8 p.m, and Jane had not arrived.

Tick-tok, the sound of high heels ascending the house's outdoor steps echoed. Jane's parents were frowning and clenching their fists. Jane rang the doorbell, but no response came from inside. So she knocked on the door. Finally, the door opened with a creek.

"Where have you been? Why are you so late? Are you seeing someone or what?" These questions were thrown at Jane.

"She was seen with a young man at Clova beach. I heard it from people," Mrs. Gomes said.

Jane had gotten fed up with this daily torture and burst out, "I want to marry, look for a boy as early as possible." Mr. and Mrs. Gomes' mouths hung open for a while. Mrs. Gomes was now sure that Jane was dating. She insisted on knowing his name and place. Jane, holding her hair with frustration, flipped her shoes in the corner. With tears in her eyes, she muttered, "Why are you all troubling me? If Jenny has disobeyed you people, why do I have to pay for it? And by the way, I don't have anyone in my life. Please find a boy of your choice."

In the following days, Gomes' family was engaged in identifying a suitable groom according to their criteria. Many relatives and friends brought marriage proposals. None of them were rich beyond imagination. Jane wasn't even given a chance to have a glance at their photos.

All the proposals were rejected. Jane suggested a boy from Parill who had proposed to her during her college days. When Mr. and Mrs. Gomes heard the name of the place, they immediately rejected it.

In Goa, people from different castes often lived in various pockets. Parill belonged to the lower-caste community. Even after converting from Hinduism to Catholicism, the four Hindu castes continued to hold significance. These four major castes are Brahmins, Chardos, Gauddos, and Sudirs. It was very difficult for a lower-caste boy to marry a higher-caste girl. As for the boy Jane proposed, he was from the law caste but was extremely rich with property. The obstacle was not his status, but his caste.

After much selection, a proposal came from a distant relative. They brought a proposal for a slim man with a pockmarked face, born with a silver spoon. He belonged to a family of higher status than the Gomes family. Jane's parents, without giving a second thought to his looks, said yes. Since the groom's father worked for the Indian railways, they lived in Calcutta, where he was posted. Though originally from Goa, it was their first visit to Goa in ten years. The marriage was set for the week of their visit.

When Jane received his photo by post, she was dejected. She was helpless and could not say no to her parents' dream bridegroom. The marriage was held in all pomp and glory. But the hearts of the married couple remained strangers to each other.

When Jane moved with her pilot husband to Calcutta, she initially mentioned the restrictions her husband's family had imposed on her. Despite being well-qualified, she was not allowed to apply for a job. She was spied on and forbidden to speak with men, even family friends. Her freedom was curtailed.

At first, Mrs. Gomes wrote comforting letters to her. But when Jane wanted to come back home to stay with her parents, they stopped responding. Mr. and Mrs. Gomes' discussion went like this: "If she comes back, what will the people say? They are giving her whatever she wants and treating her well. She is safe. The one thing she is deprived of is her freedom, and it is for her benefit."

When no replies came from Goa, Jane began harbouring a grudge against her parents. Eventually, she broke all connection with them.

"Kia! This was also one of the reasons to invite Jenny back home."

Nodding her head, Kia said, "Yes, now I understand why there are only negative talks about Aunt Jane at home."

Chapter 6

Ultimate 'YES'

"Kia, the evening of your birthday left a deep impact on the future of your parents. It was as if everything had swept away in an instant by a gigantic Tsunami.

"On that unfortunate morning, Rosemary's words echoed in Jenny's ears, 'Honey, please leave that wicked, wretched house before it ruins yours and the infant's life. From the beginning until now, I've been telling you to come and stay with us. We've always feared whether Toney would be able to take care of you. Now, you can see for yourself. Initially, when you both were in love, we attempted to convince you, but you did not listen to us. Never mind, now at least consider our suggestion.'

"That night, Jenny didn't think about herself but focused on her toddler. The following day, she packed her bags and shifted to her parents' house."

"*Shammai*! Why did my grandma speak so rudely about my daddy? Why was she pressuring my mother to leave my father's house? Who was to be blamed for all this?"

"Kia, I perceive all this happened because of unspoken love. I am not sure whether it was the right kind of sacrifice in love. I have witnessed lovers who quarrel, yet reconcile almost immediately, and some who even terminate their relationships. In Toney and Jenny's case, there were no fights and agitations. Their love was all 'Yes,' It was quiet, without conflict, and that made it difficult for me to judge. I didn't know who was to blame in their relationship, but I often wondered who had instilled the venom in their married life.

"Their first letter after eloping mentioned that I helped them, which is why I was not on talking terms with either family. But when Toney and Jenny moved back to live with Toney's family, the parents decided to welcome me once more.

"Life at Toney's house was full of the joy. Tina treated Jenny like her own daughter. The house had three rooms, excluding the kitchen: a dining room, a sitting room, and a bedroom. When Toney and Jenny returned, his family converted the dining room into a bedroom for them, moving all their belongings into provisional bedroom. They gave up the only proper bedroom in the house, showing care and concern towards Jenny. It wasn't the external comforts—they interacted with her with affection and sensitivity. Jenny also had high respect for Toney's mother, viewing her as a committed, diligent woman.

"But if there was peace and happiness at Lobo's house, there was turbulence at the Gomes' house. The Gomes' house was massive, consisting of a personal room for every member of the household and two additional rooms for the guests. Which mother would not want to see her daughter in a comfortable dwelling? Rosemary always desired that she lived with Jenny and her husband, so she could be close to her granddaughter, playing with her every day. That's why they welcomed them back.

"Every day, Jenny would spend at least two hours at her mama's place with you. On her arrival, Rosemary offered tempting things to play with, and to Jenny, expensive clothes, jewellery, bags, and shoes. But there was a catch—Jenny could only have these things when she was out with the Gomes' family, and you could only play with those fancy toys at their house. As a result, when Jenny and her daughter were out with the Gomes' family, they would look like a princess and an angel, respectively. If at all Jenny wanted to possess them, she would have to come and stay with the Gomes' family. When Jenny was out with Toney, she would look drab. To see her in two contradicting appearances at discrete events was like watching her have a split personality. No one could share Jenny's feelings, not even her friend Candy, since she got married a few months ago and was now living with her husband. Jenny knew she couldn't be sailing on two boats all the time and had to choose. Whether to be the wife of a tailor or a daughter of an official; the ball was in her court. Only then she would have inner happiness and peace of mind.

"Jenny gathered some courage one day and said to her mother, "Mama, I am sorry. I can't pretend anymore. I am glad to be Lobo's daughter-in-law and would give up living as the daughter of Gomes'." With this, Jenny resolved her self-conflict. Rosemary was not pleased with her decision. She had hoped that glamour would bring her daughter close to her. From then onwards, she was extra vigorous in presenting extravagant things and waited for Jenny to swallow the bait.

"It had been three months since Toney and Jenny had stayed with Toney's family. They had not yet baptized their child. Soon, the19th of December was around the corner, and since it was the child's first birthday, Jenny's father suggested celebrating the birthday and the christening of the child on the same day. All agreed, and Jenny's father also mentioned that he would bear the entire expense of the celebration. Her father's declaration put Toney in a difficult position, for Toney's budget to buy a gift would have been considered too little by the Gomes' family. This status disparity had begun to bother him. So, without making much noise, he purchased a thin gold chain with a tiny cross for his daughter.

"The Gomes' hosted the christening and the birthday celebration in a large party hall decorated with white fabric, making the party look as if it was being held in heaven. The expensive centerpiece in the center of the hall, sprinkled with silver and gold glitter, indicated a two-fold celebration. The exuberant illuminations of decorative lighting were fixed to make the evening brighter and livelier. The sumptuous buffet added spice to the party. The gorgeous, expensive table pieces that everyone had their eyes on were the treasure of the party. The renowned DJ in the state was the live wire of the celebration. In this glorious reception hall, the distinction between the invitees of the Gomes' and the Lobos' was starkly visible. The folks with high heels and high-priced suits were the guests of the Gomes' family, while people with economical rexine shoes and not-so-matching attire were the invitees of the Lobo family.

"The extravagant celebration was also intended to diminish the Lobo family. The grandparents gained prominence in the party rather than the parents of the child. In a subtle way, they humiliated the Lobo family before the guests. Rosemary was not happy with Jenny's decision to stay at Lobos' house. So, everything happened according to Rosemary's plan to overshadow the Lobo family with their dominance. Her intention behind doing all this was to show her daughter that they love her and her child more than Toney's family. After projecting all the show-off, Jenny did not fall into her mama's trap.

"That christening and birthday celebration made a mark in the history of the Gomes' and Lobo's family. The captured moments of the celebration would remain in their memories forever. The photos taken on the day captured the undeniable differences in the attire and looks of both family members. Having faced the internal cyclone as a family, the Lobos stood together strong since they were rooted in love. Though there were fewer comforts in the house, it was still fragrant with peace. Rosemary's constant effort to coax Jenny to come and stay was still ongoing. But Jenny would not heed her mama's self-centered appeal.

"Most of the families in the vicinity now had a refrigerator. It had become a necessity in every house. The Lobo house had no refrigerator. With a child in the house, a fridge becomes the need of the hour. Though Jenny was not very keen on visiting her mama every day, it left her with no alternative. It compelled her to go to her mama's house to store food items like milk, eggs, medicine, and other compostable items that were essential for the child. But Jenny could not withstand her mama's taunts against her husband's family every day.

“One night, after reflecting, Jenny said to Toney, “It would be nice if we could have our own refrigerator.” The mistake she made here was that she did not tell him why she was interested in buying one. Toney also didn't enquire about the need for it. He said YES to her and, without asking a single question, bought a refrigerator the following week. Jenny felt nice, not because they bought a new refrigerator, but because her regular visits to her mama's house would reduce. That didn't mean that she had issues with her; it was her way of expressing love for her husband, Toney.

“At the Lobo residence, it was evident that the baby's clothes were hung on the drying line daily. The washing stone was being used by Tina every day to wash the baby's clothing. Diapers had just arrived in the market; however, they were expensive to buy. The baby's soiled clothes had to be washed every day along with the entire family's clothes, and hence Jenny tried to give Tina a hand with the chores. Tina would not allow her to do the laundry. When Jenny was restrained from doing all the major work in the house, especially everyone's laundry, she said, “Aunty please permit me to share the burden of the house.”

“To Jenny's request, Tina replied sweetly, “If I don't take care of my house, then there is no value in me. Housekeeping is my profession. I do it to earn a living. When I can wash other's clothes to feed my own, it won't be right if I don't wash my own. Till I am healthy, I will do everyone's laundry.”

“Jenny didn't feel good about it. Even when Tina felt under the weather, she would do the housework perfectly. And with the child's soiled clothes, her workload had doubled. Jenny understood her hardship and decided to lessen her own personal expenses. With this in mind, she placed her request of purchasing a washing machine before her husband, Toney. If the refrigerator was a need, then the washing machine was a semi-luxury of those days. Toney didn't turn down her petition. He paused for a moment and said, "YES! I will buy one." She never explained why she wanted the washing machine. He also did not bother to ask why she required it. Both kept everything to themselves just to show that they loved each other.

"Almost eight months had passed since the first birthday and the christening of their child. The Soccer World Cup was scheduled that year. The draw dates had been announced. Jack had a keen interest in playing and watching soccer. He was eight years younger than Toney and had just finished his final exams for twelfth grade. He also represented his school's soccer team. Since one of the European countries was hosting it, the live telecast of the World Cup would take place late at night in India. Every house in the village had a TV set. The Lobos' house also had one, but it was a small black-and-white TV. Since watching the match on a color television set would be more fun, Jack informed his mother, Tina that he would go to watch it at his friend's house. Tina hesitantly permitted him to go. Jenny overheard the conversation about the Soccer World Cup between Jack and Tina. She asked her husband for one last favour. This time, it was a color TV set. As usual, Jenny did not put her request plainly. It would turn out to be a blessing for Jack but a torment for his elder brother, Toney. Pretending everything was fine, Toney said, "YES" without a second thought. He thought Jenny might have been missing the comforts she had in her family. He didn't much interest in inquiring about her wants. His ultimate goal was to keep her happy by providing whatever she requested. Jenny knew that Toney had taken a loan to buy these things, and he would repay it in one year's time. But he kept her in the dark about him borrowing money from his friends.

"They all lived peacefully as one loving family for a year. But there was a lot of turmoil in Toney's mind, for he was sinking into debts. A year later, every lender expected their money back. After subtracting the entire household expenditure, his savings would be nearly nil, and that would be spent on paying the loan. Though there was no interest to be paid on the borrowed money, Toney had no funds to pay back in instalments.

"Toney did not share his hardships with Jenny, just to keep her from stress. Jenny, being a magnanimous person, always thought of others first. She showed her concern towards others silently. She believed in not letting her right hand know what her left hand was doing; she even kept her husband ignorant of her munificence. Toney continued, adding burdens on his shoulders just to give Jenny a better life. Jenny, on her part, was least concerned about herself but was always worried about others."

"*Shammai*, at the very start, you mentioned that something awful had happened on my birthday. What happened?"

"Kia, on your second birthday, an unexpected disaster occurred. You weren't responsible for it at all. It was hard to understand whom to hold responsible. Before your second birthday, everything was as calm as the ocean. It was the end of the year and the beginning of December. It was nearly impossible for Toney, at the conclusion of the year, to be out of debt and out of danger. Toney could foresee the tip of the iceberg when he realized that your birthday and Christmas were approaching in the same month. "Ignorance is bliss," Toney took these words seriously to avoid the stress by knowingly living under a rock, and he didn't discuss the celebration. Everything was pleasant and worry-free till the 6th of December.

"Every week Jenny would see her parents for about two hours. December 7th was not only a visit day but also a day to decorate for Christmas at her parents' home. Rosemary requested her to assist them in embellishing the house, decorating the Christmas tree, and setting up the Christmas crèche. She appealed to Jenny to spend the entire day with them and leave after dinner. On that occasion, Rosemary commented, 'Our grandchild Kia's birthday is approaching in this month; I hope your preparations are in full swing.'

"Jenny could not answer immediately. Just to protect the Lobo family, Jenny replied, "We are thinking of having a small party."

"Her mama promptly responded, 'Aren't we and our relatives invited?' She said this because she had no idea about the celebration.

'Of course!' Jenny exclaimed. To avoid further questions, Jenny then pretended she was very busy.

'Don't make us wait and tell us about the venue and time of our grandchild's second birthday celebration as early as possible.'

'Obviously, you will be the first to be informed. Since tomorrow is Sunday, we plan to finalize everything in the morning, and by evening, I will let you know, 'Jenny replied with an uncertain voice. From noon till evening, Jenny was on pins and needles. Gomes' house was now all set for the Christmas celebrations. The Lobo's house was not ready for any celebration. That day, Jenny returned with unpleasant feelings from her parents' home.

"It was time to go to bed. Toney and Jenny, with the baby in the center, were lying on their twin bed. Jenny thought this was the perfect moment to ask about their toddler's second birthday celebration. The innocent face of the child would catalyze the discussion. In a soft, polite voice, Jenny asked, 'Honey, do you have any ideas about how to celebrate the second birthday of our daughter?' This was the question he always feared.

"Presuming she was excited to celebrate and not wanting to shatter her dreams, he said, 'YES! I was thinking of having a dinner party for our relatives and friends.' Toney did not know, and Jenny did not tell him, that it's her mama who had instigated her. Neither of them knew the sacrifices they made for each other.

Jenny felt at ease and continued, 'Where have you planned the party?'

"Thinking about his current situation and realizing that he couldn't afford a grand hall like his in-laws had for the first birthday and christening, he replied, 'We'll have it at our house, with chairs and tables in the courtyard.' Without arguing or uttering in negative, Jenny agreed, though she knew her mama would not be happy about the venue. She was very sure her mama, upon knowing this, would say, "We will have it at our place." But Jenny had made up her mind to refuse her. The discussion that night ended with a division of responsibilities for the day.

Although Toney did not know how to arrange the money for the expenses, he continued the conversation, saying, "You take care of inviting the relatives and friends, along with the menu, the chef, etc. I will handle the arrangements of chairs and tables inside and outside the house. I will also take on the entire task of purchasing." On purpose, Toney shouldered the financial responsibility.

Days passed, and on the day before the celebration, Jenny finished her assigned tasks. Toney wasn't sure from whom to borrow the money for the expenses. On the eve of the birthday, he hired chairs and tables a lower rate from a neighbour. Since Toney had previously said that he would shop early on the birthday morning, Jenny wasn't worried about anything. On the eve, he asked for the list of the things to buy. It was a long list, totalling over 5,000 rupees. It included the material and ingredients for cooking, as well as the number of gifts for the attending the party. The list ended with the names of an expensive cake and ice-cream. Seeing the list, Toney was stunned. Relying on the generosity of Raju, the same friend who knew about their plan to elope, he said, "YES! I will buy all this tomorrow morning." He did not question Jenny about so many things were on the list, as it was made by Jenny's mama. When Jenny updated her mama about the venue and time, she interfered, asking her to include return gifts for the children. Jenny's mama also advised her to include the best delicacies on the menu, as their guests were well-to-do and sophisticated. According to Toney, spending lavishly on these items was pointless; this was just the second birthday, not the 21st.

At the dawn on Goa's liberation day, December 19th, Toney left the house to shop for the celebration. He promised to deliver the ordered food items before noon for cooking and to return in the afternoon with the rest of the supplies. That morning, Toney first visited his dear friend Raju's house. Except Raju, he owed money to all his friends. He was sure Raju would not refuse him. But, due his bad luck, Raju was with his wife celebrating Goa's Liberation day. Raju's absence was the last straw for Toney. Stuck between a rock and a hard place, whether to go home empty-handed and face embarrassment or to run away from everything. Toney chose the latter and never returned home on his daughter's second birthday. No one knew exactly what happened on that day. One thing was certain: Toney was helpless and broken.

The day was dazzling. Jenny's eyes were wide open, eagerly waiting for Toney. It was noon. There was no news of him, nor had the ordered things been delivered. As the afternoon sun set, Jenny's heart pounded. From 2 pm onwards, she mistook every car that drove guests from far and wide, as the one with her husband's listed materials. Everyone questioned Jenny about Toney's delay. His family and friends tried to contact him, but all efforts were futile. As the time passed by, the chef in the kitchen grew anxious and irritated. There wasn't enough time to prepare the different varieties of dishes. Frustrated, the chef washed his hands and left the place. Within an hour, the celebration had to begin, but nothing was ready. Jenny was in tears and didn't know what to do, so she ran into the kitchen. Rosemary followed her, noticing Jenny's condition. In the kitchen, Candy and Tina were discussing the last-minute arrangements. Jenny, with watery eyes and trembling, asked, "What shall we do now?"

Tina quickly replied, "We will not let anyone go hungry. Since we already have rice, fish curry, and pickles, let's serve those."

Rosemary interrupted her, saying, "What! You want to serve such a cheap dinner to my prominent guests? They haven't come from far just to have your dime-a-dozen meals. They can very well have it at their own place."

Then Rosemary took Jenny aside and said, "I am going to order some food from a hotel. But I have a condition: leave this house and come and stay with us by tomorrow. Even if Toney returns, you will not come back here." Husband is missing and no food for the guests, so Jenny was left with no option but to agree. Rosemary took maximum advantage of the situation.

Within half an hour, ambrosia food was on the table. Rosemary took over charge of the reception when no one else stepped forward. She fabricated the truth and announced to the crowd, "Please pray for Toney's dear friend, who has met with an accident and is fighting for his life in the hospital. Toney is with him and will return late at night." Everyone believed her. At last, the birthday celebration went smoothly.

When all the guests had left, Rosemary created a scene. In the presence of Candy, Jack, and Tina, she harshly told Jenny, "Honey, please leave this wicked house before it ruins yours and the infant's life. Right from the beginning, I've been telling that you are welcome at our place. Papa still keeps the doors of our house open for you. We always feared whether Toney would take care of you. Now you see for yourself. When you were in love, we tried to convince you, but you did not listen. Never mind—consider our suggestion now." With that, Rosemary left Toney's house.

That night, Jenny could not sleep. She did not know what had happened to Toney and was very worried about his safety.

She even prayed that her mama's lies to the guests would come true, and that she might have her husband back. She cried herself to sleep. Until morning, there was no sign of Toney. She left Toney's house for good, as she had promised her mama.

Chapter 7

Lighting Candles

"*Shammai*, after all this happened, what was the state of Lobos' house? Did they know about my daddy's location?"

Shammai, wiping her glasses, continued.

The Lobos' house was in anguish. The silence filled the house, while the gossip spread to the neighbours' houses. It shook the foundations of the Lobo family, leaving them in shame among the villagers. Guilt took over the household as they switched on the TV, refrigerator, and dumped the dirty clothes in the washing machine—the things bought at the cost of Toney. No one cooked or cleaned the house; to do anything, they felt drained.

The cries of the child at night had vanished from their only bedroom. The house was lifeless. The scattered toys on the floor were missing. Candy, with the heavy heart, stayed back for two days to console everyone. All of Candy's efforts went in vain as the situation worsened, and her in-laws compelled her to come back. Tina was left all alone with her other younger son to carry the cross of shame. Her eyes had sunken inside; tears had long dried, hair remained dishevelled. She finally ventured out of the house for the first time after the incident. It was early in the morning, just before sunrise, when she went to fetch the unpolished, home-grown rice from a known farmer. On the basis of his friendship with her husband, he unwilling offered her rice.

On the same day, when the people had shut the windows, closed the curtains, and switched on their lights. Tina sneaked out of her house. She turned her head from side to side and walked in the thick darkness of night. She reached the main road and played hide-and-seek with the streetlights and vehicle lights. In the panic of venomous creatures, like snakes and scorpions, she walked along the border of the road, staying far from the open, unclean gutters. Terror in her heart and terror around, she made it to the old, rugged cross. Only once in two years was, the Holy Cross painted, and this year it was scheduled for April.

When no one could see her, she lit the candles at her favourite Holy Cross. The Holy Cross, though small in size, was placed in the engraved giant stone. She poured her heart out. She stood there, head bowed, until the warmth of the candlelight in the tiny cave dried up her tears. Before leaving, she made a promise to the cross. "If you answer my prayers, I will clean you before they paint." She did not know what to do or say. She could promise no money, no influence. Without these, she could do nothing. Only God was her option for finding her son. On that night, the darkness covered her shame, and the lighted candles kept her hope burning. She continued to light them for at least two weeks. Day by day, the number of the candles decreased.

On one occasion, she forced Jack, her younger son, to join her at the Holy cross. Facing hardship at home, he had developed repugnance towards God.

He said, "I am fed up with your religiosity. Nothing good happens in our family. When everything was going well, God had to destroy it, and here you are still praying to him."

Tina, with strong eye contact and very little blinking, held his hand, "Don't say that. We don't know what God plans for us. We are expected to have faith in the cross."

Scratching his head, Jack interrupted, "Then why do you tell me to come only to that Cross, when there are many more chapels?"

Tina grabbed four candles from the side table. "Yes, you are right. Why that cross? We Catholics prefer a chapel or a cross in our locality to pray as a group. You know that in May, we, the villagers pray to that Cross. That Holy Cross has been known for making miracles happen for ages. If your grandparents were alive, they would have told you incredible stories." On that evening, Jack joined her, but on one condition: if nothing happens after the prayers, then this would be his last visit. Tina was sure that something would take place if she lit the candles at the cross. Nothing happened for weeks. The quality of life in the Lobo family was going from bad to worse. So, she too stopped at the end of the month.

The advanced electronic items had pushed the electricity meter, resulting in an increase in the electricity bill. Jack's education fees and travel expenses to the city college were also piling up. Tina was left with no option but to sell the washing machine in a bargain sale. The burden of day-to-day life weighed heavily on Tina. She even fell ill and fought against death in the hospital. The recently bought colored TV was used to pay for her medical bills. The house was becoming spacious and lighter, but the hearts of the household were getting heavier with the absence of news about their elder son.

The Lobo family, in their own capacity, called and searched for Toney in all the possible places. They waited for some news, day and night.

It was four months later, and the day was dull and colorless. The noon was just waking up from the gray and golden morning. A man in khaki outfit and hat descended from his rusty old bicycle, bringing a ray of hope to Tina. He cocked his head while raising his eyebrows, rereading the address from the closed white envelope for the second time. He called out to Tina by her surname from the road. Tina left the rinsed clothes in the bucket, wiped her hands up to her wrists, and scurried to the edge of the road. She was all of a doodah on receiving the post after years. Before flipping the letter to read the sender's address, she recognized the handwriting. It was Toney's. Without wasting time, she tore the envelope and read.

My dear Mother,

Before I add another word, I want to begin by asking your forgiveness for my shameful and hurtful behaviour. I know that my actions have caused you deep pain and humiliation. It was not you who deserved blame, but me alone. Yet, I am certain that people must have spoken harshly about you, showing no mercy for what was never your fault—and that thought breaks my heart.

Mother, you cannot imagine the storm that was raging within me when I made that sudden, unexpected decision. I was trapped in the darkness that I could not explain. Only I knew what I was going through at that time. Please believe me when I say that I do not hold you or Jenny responsible for anything—the blame lies entirely with me. Still, I cannot reveal everything to you now, for some reason. I hope you will one day understand.

I know I have wounded your heart deeply, Mother. I do not deserve your forgiveness, yet as your unworthy but ever-loving son, I humbly beg for it. I write these few lines not to justify myself, but simply to tell you that I am safe. Please, Mother, do not worry about me anymore.

What has happened cannot be undone, but I give you my word that I will rise above my failures. I promise you, Mother that I will work hard, rebuild my life, and strive to make you proud again. I may be far away, but your love remains the light that guides me forward.

For now, I am helpless to share more about the realities of my life. Please accept this letter as my first and last until I am able to see you in person. And I beg you, please do not tell anyone about me—not out of shame, but because I need time and space to find myself again.

Once again, I am deeply sorry for all the pain I have caused. Thank you for your endless love, patience, and prayers. No matter where I am, you will always remain in my heart.

With love and remorse,

Your son,

Toney

There were tears of happiness and a smile on Tina's face because she knew that her son was alive. Though the letter did not give her much information, in the evening she rushed to the Holy Cross. The twilight was breezy, and she lit double the amount of candles she usually did. The candles, clustered together, burned faster; nevertheless, they melted together. Tina's heart, too, melted with the candles. With the drops of tears on her joined hands, she gazed at the cross, and, going on her knees, she thanked Him for granting the favour. On that day, she kissed the cross a thousand times.

The following day, in the sultry afternoon, there was a shout on the main road: "Salt! Salt! Salt!" Most of the people came up to the road with woven bamboo baskets, each could contain at least fifty kilograms of salt. The sea salt is also used as manure, especially for coconut trees. The people of the coastal areas of Goa brought the sea salt to the mainland to sell it every year. The villagers gathered at the pickup truck, one family member to purchase and another to help in carrying.

Tina walked with a basket. It was the first time in months that Tina had stepped out in her neighbourhood. Her eyes were moving all around, butterflies in her stomach as she strode to the queue. Initially, she turned back to say a half-hearted 'hi' to a neighbour. She considered him hand-in-gloves with Gomes' family. When she reached the salt pickup truck, she looked straight ahead and stood fourth in line.

All covered to protect from sunburn, the Gomes family came out of the house. On noticing Tina, they walked slowly, expecting someone to take the place behind Tina in the queue. No one arrived. They kept their two enormous baskets between themselves and Tina.

Rosemary, to provoke Tina, said, "Jenny, please keep your distance. Forget about the space—don't even share the air."These words made Tina's heart race. Her palms begin to sweat. Jenny pretended to clear her throat. Tina slightly turned her neck. As soon as she saw Jenny, Jenny said, "Hi." Tina looked at her face and just smiled.

Rosemary boiled inside at Jenny's greeting. Before they could get into conversation, she accused Tina, "Look at her, acting as if she is a saint. She knows where her cheater son lives." Folks stopped what they were doing, except the one who was measuring and giving out the salt. Everyone noticed the tightness in Rosemary's eyes and her curled lips.

Tina replied, "Please don't make a scene. On behalf of my son, I'll say sorry."

Jenny intervened and said, "Mama, I have lived with Tina. She is not like that." Pulling Jenny back, Rosemary said, "What do you know? Do you know that she has shifted the TV and washing machine to Toney's new place? I don't know what else she has sent to his location."

"Mama, what are you saying?" Jenny asked.

"If you doubt me, why don't you ask her yourself?"

Tina replied, "No, I don't know where he is hiding. Yes, I have given away the TV and watching machine—not to him, but to the buyer."

"On my request, Toney had bought them. Then why did you sell them without informing me?" Jenny asked. Now everybody saw Tina as the guilty party. Someone said, "Look at this shameless woman who sold everything. Now only the house is left to be sold."

Tina joined her hands and said, "I am very sorry, Jenny. Please forgive me for not taking you into consideration while selling." Bowing her head, and without purchasing the salt, she left the line. The embarrassment was like sprinkling salt on a partially healed wound. Wiping her tears, Tina silently walked to her house. Jenny took a deep, pained breath and closed her eyes. She said, "Mama, what have we done? What if she really doesn't know about Toney?"

"You need not get upset now. Our turn is coming—spread the papers in the baskets and be ready."

Tina came back home, sat quietly in the corner, and treasured all these things in her heart. For a moment, she felt like giving up her life, but the thought of her younger son stopped her. She thought to herself, *come what may, I will educate Jack so that he can get a good job and have a bright future.* From that day onwards, she thought only of her younger son. And if anyone inquired about her elder son, her reply was, "I don't know." She suppressed her emotions and looked towards the future.

"*Shammai*, I really feel bad for Tina. She is going through so much. She is my true grandma," exclaimed Kia, stretching her hands.

Chapter 8

Innocent Shammai

Ahem, hack, hack! *Shammai* coughed and said, "Kia, now let us go inside the house. I need to drink some water."

The conversation between *Shammai* and Kia had gone on for over an hour. Kia picked up the teacup and the jeans that *Shammai* had forgotten to stitch, and followed her inside the house, watching *Shammai's* trembling feet.

The only regret in *Shammai's* life was her failure to bring Toney and Jenny together. Her last wish was not to be held responsible for ruining their lives. *Shammai* reached the steps of the house, and Kia promptly helped her climb. Once they entered, they realised that Leader was nowhere to be seen. He was restless and could not sit still, so *Shammai* said, "He must have gone home. Poor animals, what do they understand?

Kia said, "Leader is a faithful dog. I am a hundred percent sure he has not gone home. He would never do that to me." Kia opened the door and called, "Leader, Leader, where are you? I know you will not leave me."

Shammai breathed deeply and said, "This reminds me about the faithfulness of your parents. To date, they remain faithful; neither of them remarried. Even though they haven't seen or spoken to each other, the love between them still exists. Love wounded them, and only love can heal them. If we clear up the misunderstandings between them, surely they will be together again. I tried, but I was unsuccessful."

As soon as *Shammai* finished speaking, Leader appeared, having snuggled under *Shammai's* cane armchair. He wagged his tail, came closer to Kia, and nuzzled up against her. Kia caressed him and said, "I wish that, like you, who have stayed faithful to me, my parents—still faithful to each other—may one day come together".

Their steps led them into the antic kitchen. It was dimly lit by a single bulb, with a transparent glass panel in the ceiling that let in daylight. *Shammai* had equipped the kitchen with traditional tools, giving the food a unique taste. The traditional *masala* grinding stone, earthen vessels for cooking, copper vessels, and wooden spoons for serving—Though used in olden days—looked new here. The smell of dried fish, cooked over in the blazing charcoal, made Kia's mouth water. *Shammai* went to the kerosene stove with the glass in her hand, dipped it into the vessel on stow, fetched some water, and said, "I always drink warm water. But this water is no longer warm, just like my heart, which has lost its warmth after the groundless accusations against me."

Kia's face crinkled in confusion, and she said, "*Shammai*! You brilliantly narrated the love story of my parents. You also initially stated that the Gomes family was not on talking terms with you. It was my mother Jenny who mentioned to you in her first letter, that once my parents reconciled with my grandparents, even you were granted pardon. Then what troubles your heart and makes you feel guilty?

Shammai, with a heavy heart, replied to Kia's question.

"Kia, I met your daddy, Toney, eight years ago when I ran into him in the city of Vasco. Initially, I didn't recognize him. He had grown his hair out and had a thick, lengthy beard. If not for his smile, I would not look at him for a second time. I did a double-take to identify him. I nearly jumped out of my skin when I realized it was Toney.

Toney, in a courteous voice, said, "Auntie Maria, how are you?"

"Fine, but I don't understand what you are doing here after ditching your innocent wife. You disgraced and embarrassed her in public. Now she is not even in a position to forgive you. She is in trauma."

Toney, with his disappointed face, said to me, "I never intended to leave my beloved Jenny. But the circumstances were such that I didn't know what I was doing. I became selfish. I thought only of myself and my reputation at that moment. I failed to realize what would happen to Jenny; they would shame her in front of everyone for no-fault of hers. To avoid that shame, I left my Jenny in the middle of the road. I wish I had been there to face all the embarrassment with her.

The first thought that crossed my mind was that Jenny came from a well-to-do family. She would never end up on the street. There were no 'ifs,' 'ands,' or 'buts' about it. Even if I left, her family would never despise her. I knew she loved me more than anything, but I could not provide for her the way her family could. I thought, let me go away, so she can stay happy at her parents' house. I sacrificed her because I love her and wanted her to have a better life. I decided to stay away for a few months, to work as much as I could. Once I was free of all my debts and loans, I intended to go back home. Today, with the help of a loan, I have my shop, and I've named it after my daughter, Kia. In a year's time, I will be the full owner of that shop and will be relieved of my loans. The sad part of my life is, now I have everything, but I don't have the love of my life." Toney was in tears and gasping for breath. I placed my hand on his shoulder and hugged him.

The kitchen had become a confessional. Kia took the empty glass from *Shammai's* trembling hand before it could fall and break.

Kia asked, "*Shammai*, tell me, why did my dad end up crying so bitterly?"

Shammai said, with a wobbly voice, "Kia, if I tell you the truth, I fear it may generate negative feelings towards someone."

Kia kept her hand on top of *Shammai's* hand and said, "Trust me, I will never think ill of anyone, even if that person has caused me great harm."

Shammai looked into Kia's bright eyes and saw her sincerity. She took a deep breath and revealed the truth. "Your daddy, Toney, told me he was afraid and had no guts to call Jenny immediately after leaving her. But the second day, he called her house. When he did, what he heard was rejection—from Rosemary and Jenny."

Toney's heart sank when his photo appeared in all the newspapers. The person who used to be nervous at the sight of his father-in-law must have been terrified of the police, who were looking for him. In fear, he stopped contacting Jenny. Toney disguised himself as a beggar and lived for weeks at the railway station. As his beard grew long enough to hide his identity, he started a new life in a new city. Noticing his skill in tailoring, a local clothes company hired him. With his first decent pay, he bought a sewing machine and planned to open his own tailoring shop. He lived in a small room and worked day and night to make some money.

Six months after settling in Vasco, he called Jenny's home to apologize. Rosemary received the call. When she learned Toney had called to try and revive the lie, she said, in a polite voice, "Toney, Jenny has forgiven you and forgotten you. She is now engaged to marry." These words of Rosemary pierced Toney's heart. He just put down the phone and cried for days. Yet, he never thought of dating anyone else. Every time he tried to call Jenny, Rosemary answered. He would hear her voice and hang up. As a last attempt, Toney wrote a letter to Jenny. Days, months, and years passed, but he never received a reply.

When I had met him in Vasco, I was overjoyed and told him that Jenney never remarried. She is still single and that she has not shown interest in marriage. Knowing he was doing well, I got overwhelmed. He asked me to tell Jenny that he still loved her. Kia, now you know who it was that discouraged your daddy from asking forgiveness."

Kia was still in doubt. With a puzzled expression, she said, "*Shammai*, I don't see how your reputation was harmed in everything you just told me. Whatever happened, it happened to my daddy."

Shammai placed her left hand on Kia's shoulder and her right on the table next to the bench, moving a little closer. *Shammai* had no diabetes but had a sweet tooth. The only thing she had in her kitchen that a girl of Kia's age would enjoy were some sweets. She grabbed a few from the glass container and placed them in the hollow of Kia's soft hand. *Shammai* said, "First, I never had a good relationship with the Gomes' family. I ran into Toney after four long years and learned that he had not remarried. While coming back from Vasco, I was over the moon, thinking that Toney was doing well and in a position to care for his family. But I had forgotten to consider what Jenny might feel, or whether she would want Toney back. With all that excitement, the very next day I went to see Jenny. I was at the door step of her house when her mama came out and said sternly, "What brings you here today?"

"I have good news for Jenny. Can you please call her?" I said.

Jenny's mama replied firmly, "Jenny has nothing to do with Toney and his relations."

I pleaded, "Please, allow me to speak to her for at least a few minutes; it's about Toney. If she doesn't want to hear about him, then I will never bother her again in the future."

To that, Jenny's mama called out, "Jenny, can you come down, please? You have so-called 'good news.' You can give her the best answer yourself."

Jenny was not happy to see me and, with a soulless tone, said, "Tell me what your problem is, why are you here?"

With all enthusiasm I could muster, I exclaimed, "I have a message from your Toney. He has excelled in life. He wants to see you and wants to be with you."

But as soon as I finished my sentence, she burst out, "You are the reason for all this! You helped us run away, and you definitely must have helped him disappear." I tried to continue, "Will you please listen to me?"

"No, I don't want to hear any more about him from you. He did not even write to me after he left, not even a phone call, and now you want me to accept him? No, I can't. I am happy without him," Jenny replied, her heavy heart. "Now, I can never think of him." Jenny broke into tears, saying, "What did I do wrong? I just loved him. Why did he have to punish me in such a miserable way? Till today, I am bearing the burden of his faults. Please, I beg you, go away from here. Don't reopen my wounds."

These words of Jenny made me realize the enormity of her heartbreak. Jenny's mama had never revealed the truth to her; she just kept on pouring hatred into her, like adding oil to fire. I didn't have the courage to tell her the truth, so I silently left. But Jenny's mama followed me.

"Never think of changing her mind. Once her daughter is thirteen years old, she will remarry as she wants to—she will even ask Kia for permission. There will be a line of boys wanting to be her life partner. Bye! I don't want to see you again." With that, they discouraged me from doing anything for Toney. It was like when you think you're doing good for others, but it fires back at you. Kia, in this entire episode, one thing was obvious: your mother still loved your daddy; otherwise, she would not have ended up crying."

Kia smiled and kissed *Shammai*. "I think I should leave now; it's getting late, and it's almost time for dinner."

Shammai, curious, inquired, "Before you leave, can you tell me your opinion about your mother. Do you think she has any love remaining for your daddy?"

Kia, holding the sweets in one hand and the flying disc in the other hand, walked out of *Shammai's* house. She turned around and said, "If my mother looks back on her life and reflects, she will definitely realise the truth. Other than that one fault of my daddy's, she would discover no other. I can say this with full conviction because, most of the time, she has spoken highly about him. On some occasions, she has even mentioned that I am industrious like my daddy. Through her, I came to know that he was a caring and loving man. To my knowledge, she never mentioned that he left her. She always said he has gone far, and no one knows where. To tell you frankly, she has never spoken ill of him. But grandma, many times, has said bad things about my daddy. If I tell a lie, she says I am a cheater like my daddy. *Shammai*, after listening to their love story, I strongly feel they deserve each other. And I will turn thirteen this December. Before she takes my permission to get married, I will do something about it. I won't tell her that you have told me everything."

"Okay, my love, take care. I will keep you in my prayers," *Shammai* said.

As Kia was on her way back home, a thought arose in her mind: I have a significant task ahead of me. I have only two clues about my daddy: *One, he is in the city of Vasco, and the name of his new shop is Kia.*

Part II

Chapter 9

Oh, Vasco!

"Are you Vasco?"

"Yes, I'm Vasco." said a lofty man with a grizzly, gagged beard and hair covered by an explorer's hat.

"Nice meeting you, I'm Kia."

"Welcome, Kia, to my mighty sailing ship. I shall take you on a long voyage."

"What! You are the captain of this ship? By the way, I have no plans to go on an expedition. But I do have an inquiry: Do you have any parcel addressed to me–'Kia'?"

"No, I don't think so. However, I know a girl named Kia who got lost in search of her loved ones." He extended his hand. "Now, ascend into my ship. You will definitely encounter a Kia, even if you cannot locate the parcel," With that, the enormous man vanished.

"Vasco! Vasco! Where are you? Take me with you! Vasco, oh Vasco!" With these words, Kia woke up from her dream.

The day after the encounter with *Shammai*, Kia was pondering on the two clues: the city of Vasco and the tailoring shop called *Kia.* These words had penetrated her mind and sunk deep into her thoughts. She dreamed of the explorer Vasco da Gama. In 1498, he sailed from Portugal to India and became the first European to explore India. The city of Vasco got its name after this renowned voyager. The events recorded during the day interrupted the night's sleep, and in the hours of darkness, they led Kia subconsciously to search for *Kia* in the ship of Vasco.

What struck Kia were Vasco's words in her dream: "Kia, you ascend into my ship..." She took it as an invitation to search for her father in the city of Vasco. She thought the best course of action was to first convince him to come back home. She knew it would be almost impossible to influence her mother, and more importantly, Kia was aware if she reveals the truth and breaks her promise made to *Shammai* would cause great harm to *Shammai's* character. It would be like twisting the knife in the wound. Kia's hands were tied. She could not share this with anyone. Her grandma and mother had kept her in the dark about her father's absence. The only thought circulating in Kia's mind was to bring her family together. Because of this, every move she made had to be concealed. Before she left in search of her father, she needed to gather the facts to lay the foundation for her objective.

The only photo Kia had seen of her daddy was from his wedding. Her mother had secured it in a locker insider her cupboard. Grandma had set fire to all the other photos. The wedding photo was Jenny's only memory of her husband. Kia now knew that her father sported a thick beard.

Kia mulled over the places where she might find her father's photos. Lost in thought, she sauntered to the back balcony of the house to breathe in some fresh air. That evening, while lingering on the gallery, Kia spotted Tina, her other grandma, coming out of the forest. A coiled cloth was sandwiched between Tina's head and the bundle of firewood she carried. She trudged along the path leading to the backyard.

Once Candy got married, Tina had to sell the cows because there was no one to take them for grazing. To continue her patty business, she turned to raising pigs. Tina built a jaggy pigsty using debris from the former cow shade, cementing it with sludge to make it sturdy. The pigs were protected there. With the proceeds from selling the cows, Tina bought piglets, as pork and sausages were in demand at the time. The firewood she used to cook the pig food and boil water for bathing came from the forest behind the house. That's why Tina went into the forest every weekend to gather dry firewood.

An idea formed in Kia's mind: she could ask Tina for a photo of Toney. Her plan was to draw a beard over his face so she could recognise him more easily. Since her mother only had one photo, it would be suspicious if she took it.

From that day on, Kia monitored Tina's movements. Every afternoon, Kia stayed on the balcony, watching for Tina. One Saturday, when she saw Tina heading towards the woods, Kia quickly put on her sandals, grabbed Leader by the leash as an excuse to take him for a walk, and stepped out of the house. "I am taking Leader for a stroll," she said, almost aimlessly.

"Okay! But make sure you come back early," replied Jenny from inside the house. Kia walked hastily, but Leader, not keeping up, lagged behind. Kia reached the entrance of the pathway that led into the dim, sweltering forest. She wasn't afraid because she knew Tina had entered the dense, dark green leaves of the woods. She continued walking along the uneven path, approaching the point where the pathway split in two.

She had to figure out which way Tina had gone. The sun's rays, penetrating through the web of leaves, indicated that the other side of the forest led to the paddy field. Kia took the way leading deeper into the shady, dense portion of the forest. After walking half a mile, she heard the sound of wood being cut and soon spotted Tina. At a distance, Kia unleashed Leader, pretending to chase him toward Tina. Her heart raced, and though she was nervous, she was eager to talk to Tina for the first time. However, while focusing on the task, she failed to notice a hazard on the ground. Her leg caught in the bushes, and she tumbled onto the rough land. Tina heard Kia's shrill cry, "Mama!" She dropped the half-cut branch and rushed to Kia. As Tina reached Kia, Leader barked loudly. "Leader, don't harm her. Please leave us," with a stern voice, Kia commanded. Though Leader obeyed, he began pacing beside them.

"Baby! Are you alright? Any bruises?" Tina asked, concerned.

"I am okay," Kia replied. Tina's gentle touch made Kia feel comfortable despite the prickly bush around them.

"It is not safe for a girl your age to be alone in such a quiet, shady forest."

Kia looked into Tina's eyes and replied with a brittle voice, "I am here just to meet you and talk to you."

"What! And who told you I'd be here?"

"No one. I have been following you for the last few days."

Placing her hand on Kia's shoulders, Tina affectionately said, "Honey, you don't even know who I am, and you want to talk to me? What will your family do if they see you with me? Forget about talking—they don't even want to see my face."

"Grandmother," Kia said softy. Tina, moved by her words, impulsively hugged her. Kia continued, "I know my father is your son."

Tina was perplexed and inquired, "Who revealed it to you?"

Kia answered in a soft voice, "Grandmother, one of my friend's mother told her, and she divulged the information to me."

With the silvery voice, Tina said, "You risked your life just to meet me? Or do you expect something else from me?"

Kia replied swiftly, "Yes! I need a photo of my daddy." To conceal her true intention, Kia presented her request as a longing to know her father, which wasn't entirely untrue. "I have never seen my daddy. I wish I could, even if it's just in a photo. The only one we have is in the cupboard, and I don't have excess to it. When my friends talk about their dads, all I do is cry. Please, if you give me a photo, I will feel like he is with me."

These tear-jerking words almost brought tears to Tina's eyes. "Oh, my sweetheart! Don't worry; you will meet your daddy one day. I will give you not just one, but a couple of photos. Meet me here tomorrow at the same time in the forest," Tina promised.

Kia spontaneously kissed Tina on her check and said, "I love you, grandmother."

Tina, overwhelmed with love, kissed Kia on her forehead and whispered, "Love you too. See you tomorrow." This meeting with her granddaughter made Tina's day.

That day, Kia was as happy as a lark. She was overjoyed, humming tunes and skipping along the way home. In those few moments, she had achieved twofold happiness: love from her grandmother and a promise of a picture of her father. When she reached the gate leading to her house, she turned back, gazing at the forest. She remembered the story *Shammai* had told her and whispered, "You must be the same forest that allowed my parents to meet in secret. Thank you."

Kia was a reflection of Toney, and Tina felt as if she had met her son that day. She was so excited, she didn't know what else to bring with the photos. That evening, smiling alone, humming tunes, she went to bed, waking early the next morning in excitement. On her way to the forest, Tina carried pudding and some biscuits for Leader. She left the house half an hour early, eager to meet her granddaughter. Today, she was not collecting firewood; instead, she sat on a seasoned log of a tree, waiting for Kia. The rustling sound of dry leaves rolling back and forth in the wind kept Tina alert. Every time she heard the leaves crackling, she thought Kia was approaching. Five minutes before the proposed time, Kia arrived, calling out, "Grandmother!

Grandmother!" Tina's heart soared at the sound of Kia's voice, and she rushed to meet her

Tina hugged Kia, opened the canister with pudding, and fed Kia by her hands. Kia was astonished. "Grandmother, how did you know I love pudding?"

"I guessed it. Your thinking and behaviour resemble my son, Toney. So I assumed you'd like pudding." Tina then unfurled the cloth piece she used to carry firewood and handed Kia a couple of photos. Pointing to the family photos, she said, "Though your daddy is not here, remember our Lobo family will always be at your disposal any time." Kia clutched the photos tightly, embracing Tina, who kissed her, before letting her go. Kia returned home, full of joys, as if spring had arrived.

Kia worked on her second task of inquiring about the place Vasco. At school, she looked for a chance to interact with her geography teacher to learn about its location. In the library, she was like a bookworm, opening and closing the encyclopaedias and history books that explained the history of Vasco. On the school bus, her only conversation with the bus driver would be about the safest and best route to Vasco. At home, she grabbed the newspaper from the hands of her grandpa and the T.V remote from the hands of grandma to update herself on the current issues in Vasco. She spent almost a month, gathering information about Vasco.

Vasco is a place cradled by the Arabian Sea. As a result, it had traditionally been inhabited by the fisher folk. Vasco is blessed with a natural harbour, and through this harbour, Vasco da Gama had entered Goa, giving the city its name. The liberation of Goa granted the government control over the port. All eyes were on Vasco, as it made it easier to trade via sea routes. Consequently, the expansion of the port was in full swing. Notices were sent to all the fisher folks to vacate the area. The native people were left with only two options: settle elsewhere in Goa or change their occupation. The progress reached a climax: there was a need for better ways to dispatch the stockpile at the port. As a result, a railway line was laid in Vasco to improve transportation. The more goods they received, the more migrants came in as professionals and labourers. This resulted in more outsiders than Goans in Vasco. Vasco became a hub for trade and commerce. Day by day, the population increased, and people became more disconnected. It reached a point where next-door neighbours didn't know each other. The outskirts of the city were no longer defined by the homes of the locals but by the gigantic walls of industries, which had easy access of raw materials from the port. These industries occupied the remaining portion of the city with company offices and residential apartments.

Amidst the city's growth, there was a rise in crimes and illegal activities. The number of street children was increasing. Some lived by begging and collecting plastic bottles. Others earned their livelihood by singing and dancing for train passengers. The destitute youth found at the railway station sustained themselves by pick-pocketing. The daily newspapers reported that Vasco had high numbers of murders and trafficking cases.

Kia was also well aware of the pros and cons of Vasco. To remain unidentified among the people of different walks of life is not a big deal. However, being alone in a place known for illegal activities was Kia's concern. But nothing could stop her from exploring Vasco and finding her daddy.

Kia worked tirelessly to accumulate the information. She also wanted to ensure that her mother, Jenny, would forgive her daddy if he asked for forgiveness. So Kia played a trick on her mother. One afternoon, Kia came home with a grumpy face. She flung her bag onto the bed and insisted that her mother give her the keys to the cupboard. Kia claimed she had misplaced her plastic teardrop earrings and wanted the gold ones that were locked in the cupboard. Jenny was busy with her secretarial work while working from home for her father. Her father had taken voluntary retirement from his government job because his integrity and rigidity had made more rivals than friends in the corrupt government system. With that, his association with the government ended. He later started a real estate business, and Jenny assisted him in his new venture. Though Jenny was engrossed in her work, she paid attention to Kia. She informed her about the location of the keys.

Kia deliberately slammed the cupboard door. The noise prompted Jenny to inquire about Kia. She decided to check on Kia after finishing reading the letter she had just scanned.

"You are responsible for all this. If you were here, things would have been different." These raucous words came from the room where Kia was. Jenny had to pause the scanning of the letter. She jostled the chair, then the door, and entered the room. Kia was sitting in the corner on the floor, reclining against the wall. Kia's ears were adorned with the plastic earrings. Jenny approached Kia. To her bewilderment, she noticed the wedding photo in Kia's hand—the only photo she had of her husband. Kia was talking to the photo: "I hate you. You ruined my life. All my friends boast about their daddies, and you are not even bothered about me. Mother says you have gone far, and even if you come back I will never accept you. My mother may like you, but not me."

"Baby, please don't be rude. He is your daddy," said Jenny comfortingly.

"Where is my daddy? What is he doing so far away from me?" Kia said in a taut voice.

"No, Kia, he hasn't harmed you. When you were a baby, he loved you very much." Jenny replied.

In a modulated tone, Kia asked, "Mother, Grandma, and you have nothing but scorn for my daddy. So why do you insist that I love him?"

Jenny gently took the photo from Kia's hands, stooped down, and cuddled her. In a placid tone, she responded, "Darling, as a person, your daddy was a paragon of virtues, an endearing person.

I can't forget him, but I also can't forgive him for what he did to me."

"Oh! It's good that you still remember Daddy. And if you know the truth, you will definitely be able to forgive him," Kia murmured.

"What did you say?" asked Jenny.

"No, nothing," came the prompt reply from Kia.

Kia realized that her mother was completely against her daddy. Kia felt content. She was aware her mother didn't need any convincing to talk about her daddy. The thought passed through Kia's mind: "All will be okay if I do something spectacular, opening the eyes of my parents. Once again, the air of love will blow into their hearts." Kia couldn't wait for her 13th birthday.

Chapter 10

Old Goa

Early in the morning on 3rd December, before going to school, Kia, along with her mother and grandma, left home to attend one of the festive mass. December 3rd attracted Catholics from all corners of Goa to Old Goa. It's the Feast Day of Saint Francis Xavier. Goan Catholics celebrate the feasts of many saints. Among them, this is the most prominent feast for all Goans irrespective of caste and religion. It's the feast of the patron. It's a state-level feast and a declared holiday, so it makes it possible for young and old to participate. The reason behind its popularity is St. Francis' incorrupt body, which is preserved in the Basilica of Bom Jesus. It is also a UNESCO World Heritage Site.

Kia and her family traveled on the empty roads before they became busy. Their hired car parked half a kilometre away, and they decided to walk. They walked into the crowd-filled grounds that had the *pandal.* Noisy festive occasions choked out the voice of every stranger. The Masses went on from dawn to dusk, people moving in thousands, leaving the campus hasty and dusty.

It was one minute to go for the entrance hymn of the mass; ushers pointed at the far corner that had empty chairs. Before someone could occupy them, Kia and the family rushed. It was a winter morning; however, the density of faithful didn't spare anyone from perspiration. With the prelude, musicians in the choir softened their music, drowning out the talking of the crowd outside the *pandal.* The singers in the choir created an environment of prayer with their melodious blend of voices. The incensing of the altar in the beginning brought an ethereal feeling. All ears and eyes were on the Archbishop of Goa. From the introduction to the homily, the liturgy resounded with the theme: the girl child in everyone's ears. "Unlike some conservative parts of India, here we give almost all girls education. It's not enough; we must also give them the opportunities to work even after their marriage. Otherwise, we won't accomplish the purpose of educating girls." These were the keywords of the Archbishop in his homily.

A few minutes before the end of the mass, people of other faiths, especially Hindus, remained seated, and the congregation stood in line to receive the Holy Communion. Kia kept her bag on the chair and joined the line. After she received the Lord Jesus in the form of bread, she prayed in her heart and remained standing there until the final blessing. While the recessional hymn was being sung, people hurried to view and kiss the body of Saint Francis Xavier. As if the preserved saint was going to run away, people were pushing each other. Grandma pulled Kia into the crowd. In her hurry, Kia forgot her minimalist bag on the chair. She wanted to fetch it. All the money she had collected was in it. To lose it was like losing all hope, for it also contained the photos of her father.

To secure Kia amidst the throng of the congregation, Rosemary caught hold of her hand tightly. Kia unclasped the fingers that caught her wrist with the other hand and darted towards the chair. To go in the opposite direction in the pushing crowd was like walking against the current. As soon as she reached, she grabbed the bag and turned back. No familiar faces appeared. Twisting her head, she stood still. She thought of making a precipitous decision to run towards the direction she came. However, it was difficult to find her own amidst the people with high heels and broad suits. She dropped the idea and stood where she was.

As soon as Jenny and her mother reached the doorstep of the basilica, they learned that Kia was missing. Tension and nervousness were visible on their faces. They left the queue which led to the veneration of St. Francis's body. Their hustle-bustle to enter the church went in vain. Eyes wide open, they looked for the yellow-colored frock. Their haste and inquiry were in vain. No matter how much they raised their voices calling her name, the only thing loud enough among the excited crowd was the loudspeakers playing devotional songs. Jenny dashed to the stage setup for the Eucharistic celebration. Snatching the microphone forcefully, she shouted, "Kia! Kia! Where are you?"

An attendant rushed to her and said, "What are you doing here? And for your kind information, the mic is off." Rosemary stepped in and told him that she had lost her granddaughter. An official announcement of a missing girl grabbed the attention of everyone, and all looked around to find the described girl.

Kia pushed through and made her way backstage. Bouncing on the toes, clasping her hands to her chest, Jenny sprinted upon sighting Kia. Kia, with an overall visage that glowed and with a bright smile, hugged Jenny. Jenny whispered into Kia's ears, "I will never leave you alone, and I will see that no one comes between us."

Kia, tears in her eyes, said. "Mother, I am sorry I left grandma's hand to get the bag."

"It's okay, sweetheart, but don't do it next time. If you lose a bag, we can buy a new one; you are precious—the one and only we have."

By now the crowd in the queue was smaller, and the crowd in the *pandal* was increasing to attend the next mass. Kia, with respect, placed the flower garland on the heap of flowers and paid homage to the sacred body of St. Francis Xavier. Then she lingered behind, noticing the donation box. She faced towards the casket of St Francis Xavier, stood closer to the box, and said, "I am sorry I can't afford to put this money. I hope you will understand, and you know very well why I need this money." She pretended as if she was putting something in the box. Jenny stood at the feet of the crucifix at the side of the basilica with closed eyes, praying about how to tell Kia about her decision. Rosemary, as a typical grandma, was engrossed in kissing the statues all-around the basilica and stayed behind. As a result, Kia's donation went unnoticed. Coming out of the basilica, Kia said, "Grandma, why are you pressing those flowers in your fist? You should have placed it at the casket."

"I am not pressing them; these flowers were touched to the miraculous crucifix in the church. I am taking them so that grandpa may kiss them and receive the blessing," Rosemary said while putting the flowers in her purse.

"Grandma, your faith is great. I wish I had picked some to give to my old dear friend."

Jenny turned back and said, "Who is that old friend whom I don't know?"

Not wanting to tell the truth that she was thinking of *Shammai*, Kia just said, "Oh, she is the lady who works in our school canteen, who shares stories with me."

Outside the ancient church, the sun peeped through the clouds. Streets on both sides were packed with petty stalls trying to prove which was better than the other. The vendors opened their umbrellas. The air was filled with festive perfumes; people hurried to the petty hawkers to get refreshed with fresh lime soda and sugarcane juice. At the same time, the colourful stalls of sweets and toys enticed every child. Festive fairs along the road tempted every passer-by.

"Daddy, I want this and that!" On hearing this, Kia's eyes saw a girl with her parents.

"No, please don't buy a hair band for her. She has too many. You are pampering and spoiling her," her mother said, raising her eyebrows and giving a glassy stare to the girl's father.

"It's okay, she is a child, and I love to see my princess's hair band match her outfit," said the father of the child. The love of a daddy for his child brought tears to Kia's eyes. On heavy feet, she walked, feeling a void in her heart.

Kia's eyes were not on the toys or the fancy dresses. She was looking for the boy's pants and T-shirt. She requested Jenny to purchase blue denim pants and told her that school expects them to wear one for a dance at the concert. Kia smiled and received a pair of shoes along with the pants. She also demanded roasted grams, which she loved the most among all the festive sweets.

Rosemary, looking disturbed in the car, touched Jenny frequently and signalled her to pour out her mind to Kia. Jenny appeared to be engrossed in deep thoughts and was even unaware of the jolt caused by the driver's sudden breaking. Kia's thoughts were running over mountains and seas. Even though Kia was uncertain of the outcome of her thoughts in action, but she was confident in executing them.

It was also a day of celebration in Kia's village too. The village chapel, dedicated to St. Francis Xavier, had a grand mass in the morning. Mr. Gomes attended that mass. By noon, Kia and her family members had a sumptuous meal, and in the afternoon, on a heavy stomach, she slept like a baby.

Traditionally, the folks of Goa, on the day of their parish patron's feast, in the morning have spiritual activities such as holy mass, processions; in the noon, a festive meal; and in the evening, entertainment in the form of Tiatr (drama), cultural programs, or tournaments.

Kia and her mother, clinging to each other's hands, walked the street of their village. The twilight blurred their sight of the St. Francis Xavier Village Chapel. The excitement to watch the

Tiatr was oozing out, as Kia loved acting. She was a natural actor and had also bagged many prizes for dramatics and elocution.

The time for Tiatr almost slipped by; the audience whistled and shouted in the open air to begin the Tiatr. The drama crew waited for the blanket of darkness to cover the chapel's yard. The delay was to stage the first scene with graphics using ultraviolet (UV) lights. Since they are effective in darkness, it adds to the ingenuity. Other than the creativity in a unique form, the beauty of Tiatr is also in the live music, singing, and acting on current socio-political issues. When Kia and her mother reached their village chapel, it was almost dark. Musicians had just hit the drums and blown the trumpets for the opening chorus. Externally, Jenny caught Kia's wrist snugly, but internally she knew this audience was packed with familiar faces. Here, she knew Kia would not go missing. The light effects with music, singing, and acting robbed the attention of everyone.

They based the storyline of Tiatr on a girl child living not in an ideal family but with her employer's family. The crowd was silent and in tears when the *Kyriad* (servant) was being ill-treated by the owner in the Tiatr. The servant girl was illiterate. Traditionally in Goa, people of high caste had *Kyriad* from the lower caste, who stayed with them. Sometimes they adopted them and called them *poskes.*

Kyriad cooked the tasty food, but when she received stale food in that scene, the audience could notice the tightness in her eyes and expression. From the back, a woman who was totally into the Tiatr said, "She did not choose to be born in a poor family; it is not her fault. She is working hard for the owner. Why is she deprived of basic facilities and marriage? That kind of owner should be in prison." The surrounding audience, putting their fingers on their lips, made the noise "*shuuu... shuuu*" and said, "Quiet, please."A few of them even shouted bad words at the ill-treating owner. It was a tear-jerking Tiatr.

Every comedy scene took the crowd to another level. People laughed, clapped their hands, hit others on their shoulders, and Kia had a hearty laugh, swaying her head at the end of every comedy. At the emotional scenes, she held her mother's hand tightly. Jenny poignantly did not even laugh during some of the comedy scenes. The entire day she had been thinking about how to tell Kia what she had promised her mother.

The curtains closed on the stage. People joined their hands in a final applause. They switched the lights on the ground. After sitting for a long time, some stretched their bodies, and others looked for their own to go back home. Some drove, and others walked home at midnight. The chapel being just 500 meters from the house, Kia and Jenney walked back. It was cold. Jenny told Kia to blow her breath into the palms to keep warm.

Back home, on opening the door, they noticed Rosemary bright-eyed and waiting. She wanted to ask Jenny before retiring to bed. She signalled for Jenny to come to the corner. Avoiding eye contact, Jenny said, "Kia baby, you go to sleep, and remember, tomorrow you don't have a holiday; you have to get up early for school." Kia, remembering school, made a small noise in her throat, and said, "Okay."

With eyes wide and rounded, with very few blinks, Rosemary asked, "Did you tell her about your plan?"

"No, I am not in a position to tell her," said Jenny.

"What! You told us that when she is a teenager you will get married, and she will be thirteen this month. You're just 31 and have a long way to go. Please give your ear to my appeal," said Rosemary.

Jenny removed her sweater, tears in her eyes, and said, "No, mama."

"What's the problem?" Grabbing her sweater, Rosemary asked.

"Today in the morning, when I lost her, I couldn't handle it calmly. I realized I can't live without her, and I don't want a third person in our life. I am just concerned about her future."

"Initially she will feel abandoned, but time will heal her. And you can't be there with her all the time. Allow her to be independent."

"During the homily, the Archbishop stressed educating and allowing girls to get jobs which they like. I want to give my daughter the best education, so that she can secure a good job and stand on her own feet. That's the way I want to make her independent. While this is happening, I need to be there for her."

"Yes, I understand, but at least you must know what she wants—whether she wants you to be single and suffer."

"I don't want to do that. I am happy to be a single mother. The Tiart opened my eyes to the situation of a girl child, especially when they are least cared for by the parents,"

Rubbing the back of her neck, Rosemary said, "I still want you to rethink." On that night, Jenny spent hours on the bed, praying to God over the decision she had made that day.

Chapter 11

Hi! I'm Karthick

Kia had been planning for months for her forthcoming endeavour. Being a kid, she was not even aware of the danger of being alone in an unfamiliar place. On the eve of her 13th birthday, she packed her bag and planned her venture. She was privileged to have a personal room above her grandparents' room and opposite Jenny's room. Light and sound would immediately communicate any message from her room to her mother. She didn't leave a single trace of suspicion, hiding all of it under her bad. As usual, when her mother walked into her room to give a goodnight kiss, she left with no curiosity. In theory, Kia was well prepared, but she had never traveled alone in any part of Goa; yet nothing would stop her love for her father.

Before the crack of the dawn, when the house was in pin-drop silence, when her room was still in darkness, anxiety awakened Kia from sleep. Glancing at the corners of the room and making her judgment perfect in darkness, she was out of bed. She knelt and dragged the bag out. She skipped visiting the washroom, just to avoid the light and sound. At the moment, she had everything under control; Leader was fast asleep. She disturbed him and he woke up. He growled in surprise and was about to bark, but at that moment, he identified Kia. Kia took a deep breath. She whispered in his ears, "Thanks, Leader, for being good and maintaining silence in the room." She put on the backpack, carried Leader supported by both arms, and in her right hand caught the well-worn slippers and tank top. She came out of the room and fled from the back door.

Outside, darkness and cold were making merry. She removed her threadbare sweater from her tattered school bag. The moonlight was brighter than that of her parents' elopement night. Surrounding all the houses, the lights remained off. The flickering Christmas lights outside some houses welcomed her.

She let Leader onto the ground in the backyard and marched towards the forest. Her blood ran cold at the sight of tall, unarranged formations, like a giant phantom wearing fluorescent green rings. She paused in the middle of the road and noticed no movement in her opponent. She realised that it was the path alongside the chikoo orchard. Those chikoo trees were saplings when her parents were initially in love. You can't keep a child and chocolate together; similarly you can't keep chikoos in the sight of bats. Those rings scared bats at night. Her heart beat settled, but the murk made it hard to figure out the compound's exit.

Kia had heard and read about the girl child not being safe in unknown places. In the forest behind her house, she transformed herself. The forest was cold and speechless. Every step deepened the darkness. No whisper around, yet panic inside, she proceeded. The leaves turned the surroundings from astronomical twilight to night's darkness. Sliding her hand into the bag's side, she pulled out a torch. She set the leashed Leader free from her hands to the ground. Torch in one hand and leash in another, she strode. It was the same intersection where she halted and was confused while searching for Tina. Now she had not missed the way, but purposely halted. Pointing the light into her bag, she brought out the scissors. Raising it towards the vivid blue sky confirmed the jaws of the cutting edge. Till the length of her hair reached the size of eyebrows, she mercilessly chopped them with paper-trimming scissors.

A long way was ahead to cover. To keep strong and standing on her feet, she had to feed herself and Leader. She brought out two buns. One bun she shared with Leader and the other she ate with water. Dusting her hands, gulping the bread, and sipping the water, she exhaled and gazed at the distance. She fastened Leader with a leash to her leg for half an hour. Amidst the woods, beyond the few trees in the fields, there was nocturnal twilight. Steadying her steps, she proceeded towards the right, which ended in the bizarre, claustrophobic forest. She fixed her eyes on the left side. The path gradually lit, and she halted at the bus stop in civil twilight.

The sunrise lit the view of the first bus leaving for Margao. Kia boarded the bus. Leader was so hesitant to enter the bus that she had to yank him. She occupied the last corner seat of the bus. Fear gripped her at the last minute. The fisherwoman was the only familiar person in the bus. At the sight of her, Kia broke out in a cold sweat; she covered her ears and face with the shawl. She kept Leader busy with the dog-chew under the seat. The fisherwoman was on her way to the Margao wholesale fish market. The bulk purchase of fish and peddling house to house was in her every day schedule. Kia's house was in the third row on her way to sell fish. If she had any hints, she would visit Kia's house first on that day. Kia pretended as if she didn't know anyone. The bus came to a standstill at the bus stand. All showed eagerness to get off. The last person was on the last step of the bus, and from the last seat, Kia reached the first step. The next thought running in her mind was to look for the signpost pointing out the arrow towards the railway station.

She took a deep breath when she saw the board on the train from Margao to Vasco. Without wasting another moment, she boarded the train hastily.

Even after the prolonged train horn, the coach was in forty winks. A gravelly voice requested, "Ticket, please."

Ignorant about buying a ticket on the train, Kia replied, "I don't have one. Take this money and give me one."

"No, I can't give you a ticket here. You have to either pay the fine or step out at the next station." Among the nine passengers, only Kia's eyes were wide open during the travel; now they were even wider. Aghast, Kia fumbled for words.

"Sorry, I don't have that amount of money and can't forfeit all the currency I have." The shabby pants and wrinkly, ripped-out pocket shirt questioned her genuineness. Assuming she was a purse-snatcher or beggar, the TC implored Kia to decide before the next station arrived. Leader was lying belly up, sleeping under the berth. If TC noticed a groomed and elegant Leader, he would have changed his mind. To avoid more trouble, Kia waited for the TC to move to another bogie, and later she lifted Leader. Leaning on the pole next to the latched exit, she gazed outside through the blurred glass of the window. Nothing was clear to her—whether to advance towards Vasco or end the journey at the next station.

The travellers all around, yet alone within, Kia got off at the next station. From the station's name board to the railroad, she did not know a single route. Among the scattered faces, no acquainted and friendly one appeared. Sitting at the corner on the bench, holding not even a platform pass, she spent one hour in dread. All she thought was of her parents' love for each other.

"Hi, I am Damu," a shrill voice broke through Kia's thoughts at the railway station. She noticed a lad selling the national flag on the occasion of Liberation Day, who was sitting on the same bench. He had dishevelled hair, shabby clothes, and worn-out footwear. "Have you decided not to say anything?"

Keeping her head straight, only moving her eyes, she said, "No, I don't speak to strangers."

"I may be a stranger to you, but not to the railway station, I earn my daily bread here."

"Please leave me alone."

Damu cleared his throat and said, "Okay, let me talk about you. You look like a destitute boy of about 11 years, and your dog is not a mongrel but of a good breed. You don't match your dog."

With a stern voice she said, "You guessed it right, it's my friend's dog."

"Your friend must be from a rich family."

"That is none of your business."

Though she was not nice to Damu, on noticing her dried tears he had compassion for her and said, "Here at Majorda station, no one will deliberately inquire about your story. But your face, as long as a fiddle, pleads with others to listen to you. I think through sharing, we lessen our burden. You can tell me what happened in your life, if you don't mind," said Damu. Initially, Kia gave a deaf ear to what Damu was saying. At the same time, his observations and judgments were correct. Since she got lost at the station between the train and the track, she finally unveiled herself. Taking off the complimentary hat, she had received with one of the milk products, Kia muttered, "By the way, I am not a boy, I am a girl, and my name is Kia."

Damu dragged his rusty-dusty bag to the other corner of the bench. From a distance he exclaimed, "Oh no, you are a girl! Then why did you disguise yourself as a boy?"

"Please don't tell anyone." Kia joined her hands, pleading.

"I hope you are not in a snag. Today is Liberation Day, a good day to do charity. If you wish, you can give me an opportunity to help you. And I have only these five flags to sell; then I am done for the day."

Kia doubted his genuineness, asking, "Why do you want to help a stranger?"

"I don't like to see a girl like you, homeless in a vulnerable area. Anybody can harm you," Damu said, clearing his voice.

Kia, with a tremulous voice, said, "That means this is not a safe place and I shouldn't be here. And you think I am skating on thin ice. If it is so, on what grounds should I trust you?"

Damu kept those few flags on the bench, turned towards her, and narrated his painful story.

"I was neither born in a slum nor in Majorda. Salesmanship didn't run in my blood. I was born on a farm to a farmer in Vasco. Our land was grabbed from us, and they turned the food grain-producing land into industrial estates.

Our family, with our neighbourhood, had to evacuate the place. Though they promised to provide a flat in the city, the apartment still stands abandoned. Living in the insalubrious vicinity deteriorated my mother's health, and she passed away due to pneumonia. My father is a rough diamond. The person who worked with an axe and pickaxe—what will he know about the pans and pencils? He was jobless until they hired him as a coolie at this station. I had to leave school when I was of your age. Today is a holiday from my routine job of selling samosas to the passengers at the railway station. I don't waste a single day without working, so I am out with flags to make some extra money. My father and I slog to educate my little sister. Kia, I consider you as my sister. Trust me! Feel free to share your difficulties."

Damu's story moved Kia. She felt secure in his hands. From the word go, Kia revealed the love story of her parents and ends with how she landed at the station.

Damu stood; he stretched his hands and legs and saw the clock—almost one hour had passed in talking. He randomly gave away the flags, and with Kia proceeded towards the exit. Casually he questioned her, "No one told you we have to buy the train ticket prior to the journey? Even to be here, we have to possess the platform pass."

"Oh no! I don't have either of them. The only ticket I have on me is a bus ticket," Kia said.

That was the first time Kia had travelled in a train. The only words she remembered from the school bus driver were, "If you take a train at Margao station, you will find yourself at Vasco within two hours. Vasco is the last stop on the route." Even in her dreams, she did not know about buying a ticket on the train. In the morning, from the forest through the green fields to the bus stop and in the bus, she had bought the ticket.

"So you are sitting here on this bench illegally. Come; let us go out of the station to purchase a ticket." Damu, while descending the staircase at the station, said. "You are punching a ticket to go where?"

"Vasco."A pretty smile appeared on her face. Holding his hand tight, she said. "That's so nice of you to have faith in me and encourage me. When the TC put me out from the train, I felt that all my efforts were in vain. After speaking to you, I am filled with confidence once again. And the best part is that you are joining me."

Damu fumbled for words, scratching his head through the hair, and said "I am joining you till Vasco, then you will be by yourself. I am very sorry, I cannot be with you all the time. I have work." Damu placed his hand on her shoulder with a consoling voice and said, "I will not leave you there alone. I will request my buddy Arun at Vasco to take care of you." Kia could not control her tears. With a hug, she accepted him as her brother. It was a scene of communal union. Damu, wiping the tears from her sparkling eyes, with a silvery voice, said, "By the way, how many days will you stay there?"

She said, "I don't know. Until I find my daddy, I don't want to come back. But please don't worry, I have some money on me and food. I will manage with that."

“Hmmm...I am happy and impressed with your determination. But that area is not pleasant for a girl to stay there for long without a family.”

“What! I am, girl—no! Now I am boy. And I have my Leader to guard me,” she denied, turned her face, and looked at a bagger next to the steps. “My daddy, when he arrived at the railway station, disguised himself as a beggar.”

“Ok, as per your wish. If you declare yourself as a boy, then what shall I tell Arun?”

“Tell that I am an orphan.”

“He lost his parents because of an accident. His aunt is taking care of him as if they found him in a dustbin, and not as her brother's son. He feels it is better to live as an orphan among the orphans than be treated as an orphan.”

“It sounds good. Yet I don’t understand why I should keep you with Arun rather than with me. This question Arun will definitely ask me. What shall I answer him?”

Kia urged Damu to say, “I'm leaving him with you only for a week, until Christmas. His aunt, who is searching for him like a mad dog, knows he’s my friend. I’ll be the first person they interrogate. Damu, I think if you tell him this, Arun will believe you.”

“Yes, he will believe me.” Kia, with a beaming smile, extending her hand and shaking his, said, “Hi I am Karthik.”

Chapter 12

20th Evening

Kia—now Karthik—had spent her 13th-birthday night at Arun's place, and the following evening she found herself standing on the porch, sandwiched between light and darkness as the last glow of sunset was fading into night.

Twilight had covered the sins of the shantytown. In the dusk, Kia was doubtful of the way to Arun's home. The evening breeze tickled her cheeks, and biting her nails, she stood at a junction. With a big question mark on her mind, she turned away to gather her thoughts and stared all around to hunt for a clue. Nothing was obvious under the dim streetlight. The stump of an electric pole appeared as if it were pitched in the unruly garbage bin. Kia's eyes longed to return, and Leader's nose sniffed the bin. Hands empty with no address, only the name Arun in her mind, she rubbed the back of her neck. A few folks traversed the intersection. On inquiry, everyone knew Arun lived in the ghetto, but nobody knew for sure whether he was the same Arun. With her heartbeat thrashing in the ears, she walked up and down the path.

Kia overlooked Leader's restless movements. She took him to the edge so he could answer his natural call. He did nothing, did not even turn his neck, but vigorously gazed in one direction. Kia's snivelled, miserable appearance changed when she noticed Leader's wagged tail, and he whimpered, nuzzled against her legs. Assuming Leader was hungry, she unzipped her bag for bread. The leash dropped from her hand, and Leader ran ahead.

"Leader! You are my leader, please don't leave me alone, I am not sure of the right way." Kia said while running after him.

Nobody was there to listen, not even Leader. Running, Leader halted at the edge of the bridge. Amidst the peculiarly wretched smell, he turned back and looked for Kia. Beneath his feet was the gushing sound of water, escaping the blockage to shake the flimsy, petite bridge. Kia was completely drained, panting for breath. She threw the bread at Leader and immediately stepped on the leash. The bridge had broken railings. Better be safe than sorry, Kia pulled Leader in the center. Resting on her bent knees, placing her unbent hands on her thighs, she rebuked Leader.

"Why did you race for no reason?"

Under the moonlight, she was drenched, her clothes sticking from shoulder to back. She wiped her forehead with her sleeves and sat on her knees for a while. With a dangling tongue, Leader sniffed and wagged his tail against her, as if attempting to explain. With her breathing slowed, she inhaled the fetid gas emitted from the uncovered sewage chocked with plastic. With a buzzing sound, a zebra-coloured mosquito alighted on her wrist. She realized this is the place which she had called 'playground of mosquitoes' in the morning. She had finally found the way back to Arun's home. With stilled breaths and a wide smile, she embraced and caressed Leader and exclaimed,

"Leader you are my leader, and from now on I shall follow you." She kissed him and said, "I love you. Sorry for scolding you,"

She grabbed the leash with a light heart and stood up. She proceeded through a narrow footpath amid the thresholds of huts five meters apart. The huts engaged in conversations, and passer-by could overhear drunkards' talks and heated arguments. But the hut on the left was silent, engrossed in love talks. The hut on the right, ten steps ahead, was in turmoil—abusive language and vulgar words bursting out of it. One cried and another yelled was the scene in the indecisive street and moonlight. Leader followed Kia and just about missed the steel plate that was flung from the same hut. Kia turned back to Leader and said, "Don't worry, this is our first night in the slum. These kinds of fights may be common for the people; we have to bear with it. And remember I am with you to protect you."

Though it was dark, Kia hoped for better at the end of the uneven path. Soon her eyes were focused on the cylindrical net bag containing chips hung outside a shop. Her legs quickened to the petty shop in the middle of the uneven path. It was time to shut the shutter. The owner, dead on his feet, carried the bench to a safer place and came out, resting his hands on his waist. Kia stared at the different flavoured crisps. For a while, she was lost in a thought of the chocolates, wafers, and a variety of sweets she enjoyed at her home.

The owner was a tall, bearded middle-aged man. He munched areca nuts with betel leaf, spat it out at the stump of the electrical pole next to the shop, and with a gruff voice said, "Yes! What are you up to? I am done for the day; I can't give you anything which is already stored inside."

Kia turned her face, raised her chin, and glanced at tall personality. With a soft voice pointing out the packet, she said, "I wish to have that red packet next to the bunch of lollipops."

He looked at her, and her attire caught his attention. Before even extending his hand to fetch the packet, he replied, "That one will cost you fifteen rupees. Are you ok with it, or otherwise you can choose among these—they are for five rupees."

Kia politely said, "Yes, I can afford it; please could you bring down one for me?" From the small sum she had painstakingly saved over the past three months, she drew out a twenty-rupee note. Since she decided that in case she needed to save money, she would manage with the biscuits she had packed. So, with the remaining change, she dared to buy candies.

Now the distance was closer to Arun's house. The darkness covered the dust of the sandy path, so Kia pushed aside the brim of her hat to have a better view into the chips packet. She enjoyed every crispy flake. She ambled in order to finish it before she reached. The taste of the chips robbed away her thoughts of her mission and was replaced with reminiscences of home sweet home. She raised her face to the sky; her tears captured the reflection of the moon and rolled down over the cheeks as she shut her eyes. In the middle of the path, she hooked Leader's leash to her belt's loop. She had a packet in one hand, and the other was sticky with grease from the chips. She wiped the tears away. With a deep sigh, she once again gazed at the moon. "Mother, the only thing we both can see right now is the moon, so I am sending this message to you. I love you, I miss you. I know that you are unhappy with me, but I know the joy I will have when I have my parents together. So, mother, forgive me," she said with eyes prickling with tears.

The tiny twinned houses, among many, hooked the handmade Christmas star with zero-watt bulbs in it, which revived the drooping spirit of Kia. The raised platform for the Christmas crib made clear the only two Christian houses in that lane of the slum. This season of love and hope eased Kia's heart, and she was excited to receive the Lord. Suddenly, Leader barked at the smiling picture of Santa Claus on the door of one of the two houses. Kia smiled, touched Leader's head, and said, "Leader, why are you barking? He is smiling at you. By the way, do you know every child expects a Christmas gift from Santa Claus? And I wish that this year he gives me my daddy as a gift." On her way forward she felt nostalgic and hummed the tune of *Silent Night* to enjoy her moments of loneliness.

Kia ended her walk at a plastic door. She slightly pushed, and from inside a small voice emerged, "Shuu! Please wait there. I am coming." Kia withdrew, walked away to the borewell hand pump, and stopped.

Arun, a lad with a long nose, came out and asked, "Karthik, why are you so late? I was anxious. In the morning when you left from here you told me you would be back by 6 p.m."

"I am sorry,"

"You're so dismal; are you remembering your auntie?" Arun asked with concern.

"No, I am ok," she replied, taking off the bag from her shoulder.

Arun kept his hand on her shoulder and comforted her. "Don't worry, Karthik. I am with you. I know how difficult it is to be alone. By the way, how was the day? Did you enjoy being in the city?"

"Oh! Please don't ask me everything standing; it's a long narration. Let us sit somewhere," Kia said, squatting on the floor as she began talking.

"I started immediately after you left the house. Leader followed me, and I followed my shadow, for the day was on a rise. The rough mud road surrounded by tiny shelters, smiling labourers on their way—all of it ended when the muddy path touched the main road.

On the other side of the main road, medium size structures bloomed into my eyes. Really, nobody followed the rules—they crossed the road when they felt safe. For a moment, I thought the zebra crossing was just for decoration. In a few steps, I found myself in the alleyway. It was spacious enough to let two motorbikes cross, but nothing could stop that car, which nearly hit me. Oh! At that point it was clear—not only pedestrians, even drivers disobey.

On turning back, the location from which I had come out was gone, and I too got lost among people of different walks of life in the Gandhi market. Vendors and merchants had encroached on the lane. A few of them ran behind people with their product to compete with others. One followed me and enticed me with his flowery words, and it mesmerised me to pay for the leash. Yes! It was the first time that I bought something for Leader.

'Just missed' was the expression I framed today on escaping people coming from different directions and lanes. The textile shop opposite the State Bank of India displayed the finest red and green dresses apt for this season. It beguiled me in such a way that I wanted to purchase one."

Arun interrupted curiously, "What! What are you saying, Karthik? You wished to buy a girl's outfit"?

Flummoxed, Kia fumbled, "No…no… no, it is not for me, I forgot to tell you I have a girlfriend called Kia. It reminded me of her in that dress."

Arun exclaimed, "Oh! I thought it was for you."

Kia continued to tell what happened next. "At the end of the market, there was a fifteen-foot statue of a bald man, barely clothed, with round specs, a stick in his hand. This figure said it all about the name of the market at its exit. They erected it at the center of the intersection of three roads—one as a tail and two as wings. The right wing pointed to the residential area. The left wing pointed to the commercial area.

The statue's eyes were fixed on the magnificent, irresistible park opposite to it. Duck's chit-chat at the boundary of the park pulled the visitors to the pond. Even I could not resist. I unleashed Leader, and he was free as a bird. Leader was happy as a pig in muck; he jumped and danced to the rhythm of his own woofs. Children flocked to Leader; a few of them played with him. But he imagined playing inside the cage with the rabbits. With the cookies, I led Leader away from the rabbits' cage, and also I fed him so he could keep up his pace for the rest of the afternoon.

I stepped out of the park and was in two minds. To proceed to the left way though the garland of stores, superstores, marts, and many more was the better idea than to land in the residential area. All the posh shops spoke for themselves—in the way their items were displayed indoors and decorated outdoors. It was my bad luck. The name I longed to see on the board was 'Kia.'

"Karthik! Why are you obsessed with the name Kia? Are you in your senses? This place is completely new for you and you are hunting for a shop?" Arun asked.

Kia cleared her throat and with a tremulous voice she responded, "Oh sorry! Hmmm, once again I forgot to mention that my friend Kia's daddy has a chain of shops in her name, so I was looking for those." Kia went on telling lies.

Arun scornfully said, "Ha, ha, ha! You love your friend Kia very much. When you are here, I hope she doesn't fall in love with someone else. She is really lucky to have a person like you in her life."

Kia displayed no signs of nervousness and carried on the narration, "The dead end took me to an amazing beach. At a distance, I saw barges loaded to sail. The sun was ready to jump into the deep blue sea; at the edge of the seashore, coconut trees were swaying. Leader got excited in the open place and chased another dog that was jogging along with the owner. He could not keep up with them, so he put out his tongue and went after the tiny crabs. Waves constantly echoed the uneasiness of the water, vomiting plastic, thermocol, and paper. I felt very bad for marine life. They can't speak for themselves.

I also overheard a father's advice to his little daughter and son. "It's a magnificent castle. You could build it here because the sand is wet; dry sand will not support it. Similarly, by our own accord, we can't erect anything. We always have to be humble enough to request others for help, and above all, depend on divine assistance. I wish I had my father to guide me. My mother is the one who is always beside me."

"Karthik, you told me you lost both your parents and you are living with your aunt."

Kia raised her eyebrow and said, "Yes, yes. I lost my parents, but my daddy worked in the city and could visit only three days a month, so I felt his absence a lot."

"Oh, I see."

She continued, "The time passed by. I gazed at the ocean and realized that today I had walked towards the west; tomorrow I will have to go north."

Arun stretched, yawned, and with a drowsy tone interrupted, "Nice, so you had an amazing day, many new experiences. Come, let us hit the sack." Kia was hungry as a wolf and was expecting him to offer food, and when she was about to open her mouth to ask, Arun, abruptly with a fearful face, said, "No making noise in the house."

Kia promptly asked, "Why? Yesterday we had no problem. What's wrong today?"

Arun instructed, "Today it is the 20th, and my daddy is at home resting. He was not there yesterday. On every odd date he does night duty, and on the even date, he spends the night at home."

"What happens if he is inside?" Kia reluctantly asked.

"It is not the issue of him being inside. He is drunk; he doesn't like anyone to disturb him. I am very sorry, Karthik," Arun whispered instantly.

Kia, surprised, said, "Why are you sorry for your daddy's addiction?"

"No, not because of that. Tonight, you will not get to sleep in the bed like last night."

Kia smiled and said, "It's ok, I will manage anywhere." They sauntered toward the shanty. The half-moon sky was bright enough, but today Leader's white fur was not visible for Kia had soiled it to look poor. "One last request: now you will have to carry Leader for me, so that he may not run inside. Due to place constraints, I have arranged bedding for you and Leader under the bed. Hope you will understand the situation."

She caught Leader tightly in her arms and whispered into the Leader's ears, "Leader, no making noise inside, and please behave like a good boy." Leader joyfully nuzzled her face, wagging his tail, enjoying the warmth of her bosom.

On tiptoe, they entered the silent hut. Both advanced straight to the right corner frame of the bed. They based their every movement inside on their sense of touch. All touched the floor. Shifted places with each other. Kia, along with leader, rolled under the bed. In the dark night, and in the house with the only bulb switched off, underneath the clueless bed, laid Kia famished. The silence enveloped the surroundings; even opening the biscuit packet was a dreadful act. She unzipped the bag and shared the bread with Leader. In tears, she ate the bread. That night she swallowed the tears. Leader licked her face, and at last, they both fell asleep.

Chapter 13

I Guessed it Right

The sun's rays had just entered through the corners of the hut. The outside was warm enough to leave the house without a sweater. In his half-asleep state, Pramod, Arun's father, accidentally kicked the well-worn bag leaning against the foot of the bed. A chandelier earring fell from the side pocket. He pinched the hook, letting the chandelier earring dangle from his fingers, and said to himself, "I shall not go to work tonight." He placed it back in its place and thought, 'Why would my son Arun lie to me, saying this kid is Karthik? Something seems fishy.'

Pramod grabbed salt, stood outside next to the doorstep, rubbed his teeth with it, fetched water in a mug from the tub, washed his teeth along with his face, and was ready for the day. Nobody was in the house, so the tea on the kerosene stove had cooled. The skewed table with unfurnished plywood placed on four equal wooden pillars was the only table available.

Pramod sat on a wonky stool and drank boiled tea in a steel cup. He dipped the plain hard bread into the tea to soften it. In a plastic bag, he put the brewed tea and bread crumbs to throw outside in the bin. He positioned the cup among the steel crockery and cutlery on a rickety rack, which was doing well without the unbreakable kitchen items. He did all this while thinking about his plan regarding Kia.

Over Pramod's head was a horizontally tied bamboo, hanging below plastic sheets. They covered the sheets with zinc sheets as protection from the weather. Clothes also hung there. From it, he picked a shirt and a pair of pants, wore them, and left the house.

Kia and Arun had left the house to answer nature's call by 7:00 am, and now it was 7:20am. There were still three people ahead in the queue and ten behind. Kia pinched her nose as they were advanced closer to the public lavatory. With her abhorred face, she asked, "Arun, tell me, why there is a queue here?"

"Altogether, there are five toilets. Two of them are not in pleasant condition—either taps or commodes are in a pathetic situation. All the remaining three are totally engaged every morning. And don't ask me about the bathrooms. Either the latch has come off, or the door has holes due to rust. To escape the queue, young flock appear early in the morning at the railway track, striding with mugs and water bottles in their hands."

Kia put her fingers in her mouth with great regret and said, "Actually, yesterday I had no problem relieving myself at the railway tracks, but it was not comfortable during the day, among the boys. I would have been more relaxed in the dark."

"Karthik, I understand being embarrassed during the day, but why are you shy of boys?"

Kia immediately said, "No...no... I mean it would be nice if it is dark, so we are not visible to each other. Also, other than you, I don't know anyone else, so how can you expect me not to be embarrassed?"

By then, Kia was first in the queue. A hefty man came out of the toilet. She rushed in to finish her business quickly. To her disappointment, it was an Indian-style commode. Her entire body reacted to the filth; she covered her nose and mouth with her palm.

She noticed the door bottom painted with betel leaf spit. Inside, the smell of bidi smoke lingered. She ran from the site. Arun had no words. He simply smiled and said, "You wait for me; I may take more time than you," laughing he rushed before someone else took his place. He was out by eight o'clock. Meanwhile, Kia's mind was occupied with her private agenda for the day. Arun went on, requesting her to join him in selling tea and snacks at the railway stations. She avoided it with a humble gesture.

Today, Kia intentionally proceeded north. In order to begin her inquiry, she spoke louder to compete with the hubbub between greengrocers and customers. No one gave her a satisfactory reply. The wavy whiff of jackfruit, chikoo, and papaya triggered her taste buds. She even showed her father's photo to enquire. Vendors and sellers, concerned about the first deal of the day, ignored her, and others said.

"I don't know this person. Ask someone else."

A dark-complexioned hawker offered her a sample piece of masala guava that enticed her to buy the whole plate. He commented on the photo, "His face would be clearer without the beard. With that shabby beard, he looks like a terrorist." He giggled and continued, "My only suggestion is: please don't waste our time. I don't think you will find him here."

Kia said with a grating voice, "I know whom I am searching for. You need not give me your opinion; you had to only answer yes, or no. Don't give me your advice." She hauled Leader, crumpled the paper with remaining masala, and threw it off on the wheel of his cart.

She walked into a colourful section of the market. Here the breeze blew away some petals, some got crushed under the feet of florists and buyers, emanating perfume. But Kia, engulfed in rejection and mockery, walked with heavy steps. The soothing fragrance and the call of bees grabbed Kia's attention to the Jasmines and firecracker flowers; they were on a verge of leaping to adorn the hair bun of pretty Hindu women. Kia overheard the excitement of devotees at the basket of tiny roses and garlands of marigold. These flowers were for offering to gods and goddesses. Kia remembered St Therese, also called as the 'little flower,' and said, "Please dear, give me hope to find my daddy" Her walk through the fresh fruits and flowers had nothing to reveal about the old photo she carried with her. She did not ask anyone in that section. Most of the sellers and buyers were busy in their dealings.

In the corner at the end of the marketplace, a teenager screamed to draw the attention. He displayed low-price flowers and fruits. Having no items in store, he still shouted at the top of his voice. That caught Kia's attention. She hoped to get an answer. "Hi, can you help me?" Kia asked with an appealing voice.

"Oh yes! Sure, why not? Tell me which fruits you wish to buy? Hmmm! I am sure you will not need any flowers."

"No, I don't want any of your stuff."

"Then how can I help you?" Kia was happy to see his willingness and confidence.

"Have you spotted this person anywhere?" Kia asked politely.

"Oh, you're looking for this tailor. His shop is there." He pointed his finger to the left. Kia was in seventh heaven and grabbed Leader in her arms. With excitement, she requested, "Please, please tell me where the shop is."

Noticing the well-groomed and expensive dog, Leader, he asked, "What will I get in return?"

Kia, without hesitation, said, "What do you want?"

He responded greedily, "I want money."

Kia was a bit hesitant, with a tremulous voice, she exclaimed, "Money! I have little money on me; I have only 120 rupees."

He demanded, "Today I have earned nothing; give me all the amount."

Kia made a small face and said, "Please leave 10 rupees and take the remaining amount." He took the money and asked her to walk along with him. At the end of the lane, he turned left, pointing to one shop in line, and said, "Go straight, and you will find him in shop number 12." Wasting no time, she ran while the boy ran away to the other side. The boy continued his profession as a pilferer and set up his box at another place. When she reached the end of the lane, she saw that there was no shop numbered 12 and had no words, not even to curse that boy who cheated her.

Soreness dampened her throat and lungs. She sniffled and hugged Leader. She carried him on her way. She found herself among men with beards, sickles in their hands, cutting and chopping the bones and meat. At the sight of the meat, Leader got excited. One butcher, to delight him, chucked a bit of soft bone. Kia looked right and left and stepped forward towards the man who was kind to Leader. Kia approached him, and all stopped chopping. With heavy, sharp knifes raised, all eyes with kajal rolled towards her. Fear gripped her with trembling hands, she asked, "Do you know this person?"

From a distance, a man with a white skull cap asked her, "Who sent you here? Tell me the truth."

Kia broke out in a cold sweat, with a wobbly voice, said, "No one. He is my father and runs a tailoring shop, so I am in search of him."

He snatched the photo, took a deep sigh, and calmly said, "This person looks like us, but he is not one of us. If he is a tailor, searching for him here is useless; you may find him in the south."

Kia grabbed the photo, placed it on her chest, and softly said, "Thanks for the piece of information." Leader continued grinding the bone; she abruptly dragged him out and crossed the passage. It led them into the open air.

"Akbar, why did you let him go?" a stern voice emerged from the opposite counter.

"Ali bai, it is not Abdul Aziz's photo. Even with any amount of tricks the police play, they will not be able to trace him"

In the scourging sunlight, she walked for about a kilometre, all broken, and had lost faith in the photo. The broad, tall staircases of a fane gave space for beggars to sit on every alternative step. Pauper Kia was one with them. Biting her nails with watery eyes, she placed the photo in the bag. The beggars, with famished stomachs and pumping throats, were virtually devouring the biscuits from Kia's hands. Her compassionate heart forgot her own hunger and fed both the beggars by emptying the packet. And Leader enjoyed the last bread. Three days' dust had formed a layer on her blue jeans and white T-shirt with black fine strips. Devotees dropped coins next to her. She smiled at them with humility. Kia left early, before the sun fell, to wash her clothes and take a shower. She dusted her back, offered the coin to a beggar, and took her leave.

"Arun, I want warm water to take a shower. It has been three days, and I am stinking." Kia said breathlessly after reaching.

Arun replied politely, "Karthik, we have a head bath only once a week; on the other days, we just wash our hands and legs."

"What, only once a week? Then how come you look fresh today?" Kia pinched his black T-shirt and questioned.

"Yes, I had a shower today. It was with the cold water at noon. If you wish, you can take a bath in cold water daily. But I am sorry to tell you, Karthik, we can't afford warm water showers every day."

Kia gently said, "I am sorry for bothering you. I understand; I will manage with tap water."

Arun scratching his head, raised his eyebrows, and said, "Since the bathroom is outside our house, there is no electricity connection inside. Take a candle and hope you don't have claustrophobia."

Kia breaking her knuckles and said, "Please stay outside the bathroom and don't go away. I will just have a quick wash."

Inside, the lit candle chased the darkness but left shadows. Even her reflection in the water tub scared her. On dipping her hand into water, her body hair straightened. The puny walls of the plastic sheet and floor of pebbles increased the risk of destruction on that windy night. She trembled like a leaf because of the cold and, instead of washing herself, she put her soiled clothes in the water and wore the other set of clothes. She came out as if she not afraid and hung her wet clothes on the drying line.

Pramod stepped out of the house humming, whistling, singing, and, with his husky voice, commented, "Ha haha, you are clean and nice. Tonight, you sleep in the bed, and I will sacrifice my pillow for you."

Kia tightened her fist, baffled by his comment. She said, "Hmm, uncle, I am ok to retire on the floor; please don't take trouble for me."

He said with a broad smile, "Arun, now it's your job to convince your friend."

Kia took a few steps closer to Arun and whispered, "Why is your daddy so good to me today? Yesterday he did not say a word to me. And how come he is at home? You said on odd numbers he works at night, and it's the 21st today."

Arun blinked his eyes and said, "Even I am surprised. The person who drinks like a fish is a different person today. He has become sober. Karthik, my humble request is that just obey what he says; something in you might have inspired him."

Pramod came at the doorpost, pointing the knife, and said, "Come inside. We will have congee with pickle; it is okay if you come wearing sandals."

Kia kept her hand on her head and whispered, "Arun, what exactly is happening? Knife in his hand but smile on his face—I think something is cooking in his mind."

Arun said, "I am not sure if he will cause us harm."

On entering the house, Kia said, "Oh, he is chopping cucumber, that's why the knife. Yes, Arun, you are right; I am not even acquainted with him, but his heart seems merciful, though the actions are dreadful."

Arun softly said, "This kind of warm invitation for food I hear from his mouth for the first time," Pramod washed his hands and said, "Sita, please arrange the food fast. The children must be hungry," Sita, Arun's mother, was tired after a long day, so she said, "Please help yourselves, take as much as you want, but don't waste."

The warm, dry cow-dung floor made Kia feel at home as she sat to eat warm food after a long time. That night, the insects and flies revolved around the only bulb in the house, which burned brightly. Kia watched her plate for any that might insects fall. She had no reason to forget that night enjoying dining, sleeping, and sitting in one room. She gulped her food and burped after dinner.

"I have something else for you guys," Pramod said.

The environment in the house melted Kia's heart, and excitedly she said, "Uncle, I will have two of them."

"Yes, why not? You can have all four different flavours of candies," Pramod replied with a smoky voice.

Kia looked for a picture of Jesus to say good night. What she found were pictures of gods' posters on the zinc sheets. Yet, that night she hit the sack with relaxed muscles. The light was off, night had grown mature, silence had seated in the arms of darkness, but a single puff could wake the silence. A hand started caressing Kia. She jumped and, without thinking, screamed. She was scared and did not know what to say. All ear drums banged. Amidst the profound darkness, a voice said, "Don't worry; she must have had a nightmare." Holding her breath, she cringed. Soon after, someone whispered to her, "I was taking the candy that had fallen out of your mouth."

Pramod was delighted and said in his mind, "Yes! I guessed it right this morning."

Chapter 14

Label

Early in the morning, at the bazaar, dogs wagged their tails. They sniffed at the aroma of fried food, their salivated tongues hanging out. On their paws, they bided their time to catch the last bite of bread thrown at them by customers. The cart with bicycle wheels was the center of attraction among all the other carts. A middle-aged man at the cart, batter splashed all over on his T-shirt, catered to the hungry stomachs waiting in line for breakfast. Kia, finger in her mouth, stared at the buyers with hungry eyes. She loitered around the cart, hoping someone would bless her with pav-bhaji (bread and vegetables) or at least a samosa.

The man dipped the ladle into the vessel, its brim and sides covered with dried droplets of batter, and placed the mixture of *kanda bhajiya* (battered onion) into the greased *kadai.* He raised the ladle, pointed it towards Kia, and said, "Please don't distract my customers. If you wish to order something then do so; otherwise, leave the place." Kia bowed her head, wrapped arms around herself, and departed.

A young man, second in line, said, "I know what he wants. Please give him two samosas, and I will pay the bill."

Kia turned, her face glowing with an innocent smile, and while receiving the offering she asked the vendor, "Sir do you know this person?" Her daddy's photo was turned towards him.

"Now you don't waste my time. No, I don't know him. The favour he has done is enough; now you may leave," the vendor said with a pinched expression.

Recalling her previous experience, Kia's heart leapt with fear. She kept the photo back in the bag and asked, "Okay, fine, but do you know any tailoring shop called 'Kia' in this locality?"

The vendor looked at her and ignored her question, "Don't you understand my language?"

The young man in white shirt and black tie said politely, "*Beta* (son) you will not find tailoring or textile shops here. Walk to your right for about fifteen minutes; there you will get some laundry and textile shops. If you inquire there, someone will surely help you."She thanked the young man, who had provided her breakfast and answered her question.

Before the first bite of the second samosa, Kia thought of Leader. He was so busy eating the bread that came with the samosas. She pulled him forcefully. They turned right and continued walking. While walking, she lingered, looked right and left at the shops for a clue. Her attention was neither on the photo nor on Leader; it was only on the titles of every shop.

The dragging cracked sound of shop doors opening and the fragrance of joss sticks erected before gods at the start of the day. Products dusted and displayed as business began. All these lit a spark of hope in Kia's eyes. After a walk of fifteen minutes, the scenario changed. She found shop owners holding newspapers in their hands. Some were ordering tea and others having breakfast, simultaneously, ready to serve customers. Observing all this, Kia's heart relaxed and she hoped to encounter her daddy at one of the shops.

Shiv Laundry grabbed Kia's attention. She moved close to the shop. Rotating her head, she glanced inside and noticed hands folding and packing the ironed clothes. A red thread was tied around one wrist. "Yes! How can I help you? Have you come to collect your clothes?" an elderly man asked.

She bent her knee to climb the next step, and with a soft voice, said, "No. But yes, I want help."

"What did you say?"

"I want your help," Kia said louder.

"Oh you want help. In what way can this old man help?" Her shabby T-shirt and dusty sandals made him hesitate. He said, "I don't think I have any unattended children's outfits to give you."

"Sir, I want nothing from you, but just a piece of information"

"What formation do you want"?

"I want information, not formation," Kia said, raising her voice.

"Oh, I see. What information are you seeking?"

"In your vicinity, do you know any tailoring shop named 'Kia'?"

"What! I don't understand what you are saying. You mean you are looking for a tailor?" To make herself audible, she moved into the shop. Leader was lingering on the last step, tempted to continue toward the bakery. She attempted to pull him inside. "Please wait a minute; there are ironed clothes here, and I don't want to have any fur inside." To keep Leader busy, she put out his chew and left him on the last step. She marched closer to a bald man with a wrinkled face, white stubble beard. A thought provoked in her mind, *I doubt he will know.* While his hands continued packing, he stared at her. She said, "I was asking you whether you know a tailoring shop called 'Kia.'"

"See, dear, other than laundry, I don't take any other contracts, and if you want to stitch shirts, go further right."

With a pinched, tension-filled expression, she said, "Everyone said to go right."She couldn't look him in the eye, for something was troubling her. She was in two minds—whether to continue the conversation or move on. Then, her eyesight fell on the calendar, and she realised that she was losing days. She turned back with tears in her eyes and wanted to tell the truth. She closed her eyes, took a deep breath, gazing at the 22nd December on the calendar, and said, "Yes, I want a favour from you: to locate my daddy."

The old man's heart melted and his tone changed. "Oh! My child please don't cry, tell me in what way I can support you, or if you have any clue,"

"I saw the name Kia for the first time on the label attached to the collar of a shirt at my *Shammai*'s house."

"Okay, I understand you want to check the shirts of my customers. Well! You can." Kia kept the backpack at the corner and was about to touch the first shirt when she heard the words, "Please wash your hands first." Kia made the utmost use of the wash room and came out feeling relaxed.

The edifice was spacious, and they had laid all the clothes out according to the names of customers. The shirts on hangers had nothing to offer Kia; all the tags spoke of their brands. With her whole heart and mind, she carefully went through all the clothes at her disposal. In the end, she found nothing and she said, "Sir, I have found no clue. Now, I don't know what to do."

He rubbed her back. Eyes narrowed, eyebrows pulling down in concentration, he said, "Dear don't lose hope. I still have hope in the laundry man from the south, who will be herein half an hour. He is always delayed because south is the hub of fashion."

He offered her a chair; she constantly dangled her lag and prayed in her mind. She did not open her mouth. In that silence, the ceiling and corners spoke to her of cleanliness. She glanced at her clothes and felt like fish outside the pond. Bending her neck forward, she said, "Sir, it's okay. I am going now."

"Now, you have already waited for 15 minutes. You should wait for another 10 minutes, and by then, he will be here." She rested her chin on her palms and placed her elbows on her thighs, looking down.

A young adult came with a load of clothes. He left his footwear outside and rolled the bundle into the room. "Dear, come and please check in this batch," the old man called out. Kia jumped from the chair, but after going through every collar, her face drooped. The laundry boy had a vague idea of this shop called Kia; he happened to search through the bundle of trousers, and there he was, lifting a black pant with the label "Kia." He exclaimed from the inner room, "I got it! I found it!" Kia was about to walk out when she heard his voice. She jumped in joy. Her eyes sparkled and gleamed. Kia wrote the address on a piece of paper and, shaking her head, read it loudly. She almost learned it by heart.

When she reached the doorstep, she gaped. Leader wasn't anywhere, so she cried out, "Leader, where are you? Leader, Leader!"

She heard a casual voice from the opposite side of the road. "Are you calling out for a dog?"

With teary eyes, she said, "Yes, sir, that's my pet. Please, can you tell me where he has gone?"

"Five minutes back, there was a pack of mongrels growling at the lonely Pomeranian. I thought they were playing with the bone, but after some time, the Pomeranian tried to peep inside. On that move of his, they all pounced on him. With that, he ran for his life with the bone," Kia ran in the direction which he pointed.

Kia wiped her tears and doubled up. She barged into the shops to inquire, and one said, "Yes, a bunch of dogs went straight just now." She halted at the three-way junction and scratched her head, biting her nails. The barking dogs in the distance took her attention. Holding her loose footwear tightly in her hand, she ran. At that spot, the pack of street dogs was having a party at the garbage bin next to a museum.

Kia caught the backpack by stripping and swigging. All the beasts dispersed, leaving the excavation in the garbage bin abruptly. She broke at the site. Leader's chew, torn apart, she took it in her hands. She shook from her feet and collapsed on the ground, kept her hands on her head, and cried bitterly.

The tourists around the state museum were engrossed in clicking selfies. Some pouted before the camera, and others shouted in excitement. The children howled, stretched their hands towards the helium balloons and ice cream stalls. They dragged their parents to buy their favourites. In all this, Kia remained unnoticed, but with a sorrowful face, she looked around for another hint of her beloved dog.

With heavy feet and a heavy heart, the rest of the day went by with the address in her bag and the chewing bone in her hands, in search of her beloved. No one told her about the dog, but one foreigner said, "Not your pet, but I think you're lost," and he laughed. With those words, she came to her senses and realised that she had lost her way back home. Fear crept into her heart. No companion to sniff and pull the leash back home. The evening was on the verge of enveloping the day, and her stomach growled. She did not know her present location. She asked the flock on the way for directions to *Nakiar*, and no one answered. She felt as if she was on another planet. At that twilight, Leader was not with her to guide her back home.

When night engulfed the day, the volume of silence increased, and the dwellings almost turned off into sleep mode. Kia's face was wet with tears. The only comforting loud sound she heard was the horn of the train. That assured her of the presence of people. To look for the ray of hope at the station, she rushed in its direction.

At the station, she heard no blowing of the horn. The tickling sound of the clock was distinct and clear; it was time to hit the sack. The oscillating noise of the unattended ceiling fan had no one to frighten. The benches were cold. The lavatory had a long day, and odour would hang on till dawn. Kia's expectations shattered. With the dried tears on her cheeks, she loitered around, yet found no company. The garbage bin by the side of the canteen had some food. Though the food was stale and stinking, she swallowed it with the leftover water from various bottles. Far in the distance, she heard the train chaff. She raised her eyebrows, took a deep breath, and by then, the train approached. She waited for chafing to stop. Unfortunately, it continued and ignored the insignificant station.

Kia, head down on her lap, sat at the corner bench. The sound of mumbling and thrashing of plastic emerged from the railway tracks. A teenage girl and her mother were picking plastic on the platform. Loads on their backs went on increasing as they moved along the tracks. Kia jumped out of the platform, swiftly reaching the spot. She almost broke her knuckles and dared to look at the mother. The mother said, "Hey, young lad! What are you doing so late at the station?"

Kia replied, "I am lost, and don't know the way back home."

"What do you mean you don't know the way? Aren't you from this place?"

"No, I have come over to my friend's house for Christmas vacation."

"So, what have you decided now?"

"I don't know."

"Come join us in filling the bags with plastic bottles and other plastic waste."

"Oh, so nice of you, you work to keep the city clean."

"No, we don't work for the city. We work to feed our stomach."

Kia, for a moment, kept silent and then said, "But after helping you, where I will go?"

"You can rest at our place tonight." Kia's heart beats lowed and she smiled at her daughter. The 12-year-old daughter was reluctant to smile at a boy who was a stranger. Kia helped them to fetch the plastic, which was at a distance.

Past midnight, their mission was accomplished, and the railroad was left only with papers. They hopped over the railings next to the tracks and landed at the shelter—it was without walls, roof, and door. The moonlight brightened the night, and the cement pipes in which they dwelled did not require lights that night. Kia could hear mice squeak throughout the darkness in another pipe. Ignoring the mosquitoes' distractions, the other problem was the trains running every hour. Kia's exhaustion could resist the many sounds. So, she dissolved into a deep slumber.

In the morning, her vision was clearer, and the huge cement pipes on either side of the path were visible. Labourers from the slum traveled through a shortcut path among the scattered cement pipes. The passer-by woke up almost all the fifteen families that were sheltered in the pipes early in the morning. These broken waste pipes had built a community of the destitute. The life of these people was hand to mouth; no one worried about hiding the treasures. They were people of faith in God.

The hustle and bustle of the surroundings could not disturb Kia. But the memories of Leader compelled Kia to cry bitterly and wake up in tears. She wiped her face and was out of the dwelling. She was glad to see the person who helped her last night. The mother greeted her, "Good morning! Hope you had a sound sleep."

Kia's smile on her face said, "Good morning! Yes, I slept well"

"Take this tumbler and wash your face. Is it okay with you to use charcoal to clean your teeth? If so, you'll find it under the clay pot"

Kia made an ugly face while rubbing charcoal on her teeth, and spat it out, and said, "Yes, I am done."

"Now, what is your next plan, or do you need any help to reach your home?"

"I will find my way," Kia remembered the address she asked. "Can you please help me with this address?"

Without glancing at the paper, the woman looked at Kia and said, "Can you please read it for me?" Kia read the address. The woman exclaimed, "Yes, I know the place. It's in the south. The best way there is along the railway track. After an hour's walk, you will reach the outskirts of the city. From there, anyone will help you locate the shop."

Kia's face glowed, and she was eager to leave the place. No jam, no butter. She gobbled the dry chapati and enthusiastically said, "Auntie, let me say thank you to your daughter. Where is she?"

The woman said, "Yes, she is not here. Early in the morning, she goes to distribute the newspapers. After that, she goes to the public school."

Taking a step back, Kia said, "School?"

"Yes, she has a great desire to study, and I support her in whatever I can. We both work at night, so we are the first to collect the bottles, and in the morning, I work as a housemaid."

"What about her daddy? Where is he?" The tears rolled from her eyes. "He left us because I gave birth to a girl child. I had to leave his house and come to the city, at least to do some housework to raise my child." Kia was impressed by the audacity of that lady and the willpower of her daughter. Their story gave courage to Kia. She thought to herself, *now I will face the consequences of being a girl.* She opened her bag and wore the beads necklace, pierced the earrings, and inserted plastic bangle. In a girlish way, she hit the rail road.

Chapter 15

A New Discovery

The Gomes's house was in turmoil; everyone was down in the dumps. Every ring of a phone and knock at the door would raise hope. The teddy bear was still sleeping in Kia's bed; school books, shoes, and socks were discussing the silence in the room. Chocolates and ice-cream had no demand, but the refrigerator was filled with leftovers as none had any appetite. The night had its own dreadful narration to share, which seized the rest of their nights. Dust had settled everywhere.

There was no news of Kia. Jenny, with her dishevelled hair, took the previous day's newspaper and said, "Papa, this black-and-white photo, I think, is not doing enough to grab the attention of the newsreaders. We have to do something."

Her father took off his specs and said, "Today is 23rd, right?"

"Yes! And it has been five days," she whimpered.

"Yes, my child, I have placed a bigger, coloured photo in today's paper." Jenny rushed to the front gate to fetch the newspaper, swiftly flipped the pages, paused abruptly, embraced the picture weeping as she proceeded to the main hall and said, "I can't live without her. I want her back. I don't know what she is doing, and what she is eating, and how she is living." She walked closer to Papa; with watery eyes she said, "Please, papa, do something."

He hugged her and said, "My dear, don't lose hope, we will find her."

Jenny rested her head on his shoulders and asked, "Papa, Kia was close to you more than mother. Did she ever complain about me to you?"

"No, never. She was proud of you, and whenever you were under the weather, her face would be small. She would come and tell me, 'Please take care of my mom.'"

"But why, Papa, did she leave me without saying anything? If she loved me so much, why would she do this to me?"

"Jenny, please be courageous."

Papa looked at the coloured published photo, hitting his forehead with his palm. He said, "My dear, where to search for you? Neighbours, friends, and relatives know nothing about you, even your close school friends." He kissed the photo and said, "We love you and will not let go of you." He turned towards Jenny and said, "Did you hunt for any evidence in her room?"

"Yes, on the day she went missing, I did my best to discover at least some indication of her intentions in the room. All my efforts went in vain. One thing surprised me—she left the clothes, bags, and shoes here. Only the old items are missing."

"What can be the reason for her to carry only the bumped clothes and things?" Papa asked. "Even I am confused." Papa ran his hand over the photo, paused for a while, and said, "If we display this photo in the newspaper, then obviously people will fail to identify her. Here she looks like a princess."

Rosemary overheard their communication and walked in the hall. Carrying three cups of boiling coffee, she said, "Jenny, did you tell Kia anything about your absconding husband?"

"No, not much in detail, but she has been asking about him."

"Oh! That means what I am thinking is right."

"What are you saying?"

"I am sure your husband is to be held responsible for all this."

"What do you mean? Don't blame him without any proof."

"He might have met her somewhere at school and must have influenced her."

"I don't think so. He has never contacted me, and we don't even know where he is."

Mama scratched her throat; she raised her voice and said, "No, no, we must complain against him to the police. I am sure this is his doing. Who knows, even his family must have been part of such an act."

"Mama, please. It is our fault because we didn't understand what our child wanted. I know Tina is not so mean; she is a God-fearing person. Even though I don't speak to her, there is always a smile on her face for me."

"Tell me then, how it is possible for an innocent, timid Kia to leave the house with no one's support?"

Jenny joined her hands and said, "Please, mother, don't jump to conclusions with no evidence."

The ball of silence dropped; the fragrance and sound of coffee being sipped dominated the room. From time to time, the rustling of the newspaper interrupted the monotony. Shut windows blocked the fresh air, so the fan was tirelessly working to keep the room cool. The flower vase next to the Bible and altar had withered. On the floor, the petals moved with the fan's breeze. The seating room was full of breath but had no life. Papa, on the rocking chair, broke the silence and said, "We have no time to prove to each other, so it's better not to blame each other."

The full-size colour photo spread the news like wildfire. None of the family members could explain the situation, for all these calls were only for inquiry and did not carry any information. They got fed up with receiving calls. Though Jenny was sitting next to the telephone, she was frustrated and reluctant to take the calls. But to her surprise, one phone number persistently called them. Jenny, all set to give a firm answer, received the call. "What is your problem? Why are you calling continually?"

"Please listen to me. I have very important information for you. I saw your ad in the newspaper. I haven't found your daughter. I am sure you are Jenny, and I understand what you must be going through. I am Rita from Vasco. It surprised me because I found the dog that is in the picture."

"You found Leader? Then you must have also seen my daughter. How is she?"

"I am sorry to say that there was no one with the dog. The street dogs chased him; since it looked like a domestic dog, I rescued it from the mongrels."

"Oh, then where is my daughter?"

"I am sure that your daughter is in Vasco."

"Why Vasco?" Jenny said, surprised. Rosemary overheard and said, "Yes! I knew I was right."

"You heard right; she is in Vasco," Rita said. Jenny shouted, "Mama, please let me listen," and continued, "Yes, pardon me, please"

"I said, I found your pet outside the Marine Museum in Vasco. You need to narrow down your search to Vasco."

"Sure, we will first inform the Vasco police."

"I am a little busy, so come tomorrow to take your pet. I will be next to the museum gate."

"Sure, see you tomorrow. Thanks a lot."

Clasping hands on her chest, Jenny said, "Papa, come, let us leave right now to Vasco to fetch Kia."

"Jenny, Vasco is not a tiny city like Margao. Half a day will not be sufficient. Even if we leave early in the morning, we will have to take some of our relatives with us and spread in pairs to search for her."

"But papa, I can't wait. I want to see my child now."

"My child, this isn't a walk in the park. We have to prepare ourselves with all the details. So today you make all the things ready."

Jenny, cocking her head, raised the eyebrows, turned towards Rosemary, and said, "But Mama, where did you get the information that she is in Vasco? Who told you?"

"Because Toney has settled there."

"What! Toney is living there? Who told you that?"

"I read the address on the letter."

"Letter? What letter and whose letters? What are you trying to say Mama? Say it clearly. Please tell the truth."

Rosemary said, "I am sorry. A couple of weeks after his disappearance, Toney had written letters to you, but neither did I open them nor did I hand them over to you." Jenny's lungs constricting, making it hard to breathe, said, "Mama, what have you done? Why did you ruin my future?"

"Please, my child, forgive me."

Jenny, with tears in her eyes, asked, "Mama, what did you tell him about me?"

"I told him that you are happy without him."

Jenny said, "Mama, why did you tell a lie? Don't you want to see your daughter happy?"

Rosemary, with a small face, said, "I was afraid that you may go back to their house, and I wanted you to live happily by remarrying. Please forgive me, my child."

Jenny's father intervened. "I understand, Jenny. Your mama committed a mistake because she loved you, but I don't understand why your husband had to take away your daughter in such a way."

"Papa, you too think that Toney has taken Kia?"

"Obviously, it is his work. Otherwise, how will our Kia go so far?"

"Papa, I don't believe he will do such a thing."

"That means you still don't believe that he left you alone on the second birthday of your child."

"Please, Papa, let us hunt for Kia first, then will see what we can do about him. If he has taken Kia away, then I will never forgive him."

"We have to complain to the police that Toney is likely involved in her abduction."

Papa kept the empty cup in the tray, raised his head toward Jenny, and said, "Dear, I understand your feelings, but I can't stay quiet. Can you please give me Toney's photo?"

Jenny plodded to her room. She explored the cupboard from top to bottom. The only photo she possessed had gone missing. She rushed to the drawing room and said, "Mama, did you take Toney's photo?"

"No, I haven't touched the photo."

Papa, with his harsh voice, said, "Yes, here is the truth, and Toney's involvement is definitely proven. Kia must have taken the photo to confirm if he was her real father."

"If that is true, then where did he meet her?"

Biting her lips, Jenny said, "Most probably he met her outside her school. I never expected this from him."

Taking a deep breath, Rosemary said, "Thank God, at last you believed us."

"Yes, mama, you were right. I will never forgive him,"

"Jenny, so you don't have a single photo of Toney?" her father asked.

"I think I have a passport-size photo in my purse," Jenny said. "Please fetch it; we will have to search for them together."

"Papa, why can't we look for Kia first and then Toney?"

"If he has taken her, he will hide her with him. So the hunt for both is essential."

The ray of hope entered the house. No more arguments. The latest news kept everyone on the edge. Leader was out of the scene, though he was the first and only clue. The waiting household felt heavy every hour. The opened cupboard, pulled drawers, scattered clothes, half-rolled mattress, and the broom under the bed gave nothing away.

Papa dialled his Vasco contacts to spread the news. Now the altar was adorned with fresh garden flowers and new candles. In the evening, the acquaintances made the noise in the house, pumping hope into the hearts of family and assuring their accompaniment for the next day.

In the chilly dawn of December, the warm hearts of everyone at home were burning to leave the house at the crack of dawn. A hot cup of tea and bread with butter made it all easy. No hustle and bustle appeared among them, for all were ready to find Kia. Three cars hit the road, invoking the blessing of Almighty on the way and on the rest of the day.

Chapter 16

St. Anthony

When Kia went missing, everyone in the village looked for clues. Every meeting point in the village echoed her name and questions related to her disappearance. Many cooked-up stories were coming to light. Among them, one even said that the devil must have abducted her. Five days passed and no evidence was discovered. The investigation moved deeper and deeper.

The backyard of *Shammai's* house was dull and gloomy. Her regular visits stopped. The fallen dry coconuts in her compound were untouched. All flower-producing plants had said goodbye and the garden had overrun with weeds. The dry leaves danced to the rhythm of the noon breeze. *Shammai* spent most of her time in her bedroom. She was afraid that Kia had gone missing because of what she had told her.

In her bedroom, she kept St. Anthony, yet he had not interceded with God. On the 23rd morning, after her personal prayer, *Shammai* sat on the hard mattress bed, placed her hand on forehead, and gazed at the tied statue of St. Anthony. With a taut voice, she said, "Our ancestors believed that whenever they lost anything, they bound you with thirteen rounds of string. It is said that you perform miracles and find lost things. Now it has been five days, and no news of Kia has reached our ears. Please don't force me to doubt you."With sorrow in her heart, she banged her head at the feet of the statue and said, "And I have a humble request—please see that I am not dragged into this." Her pet cat licked her face. She was in qualm whether St. Anthony would really hear and act upon it.

Shammai's house was on pause. The quality of food in her house had also reduced. Fisherwomen who went house-to-house selling fish missed the last few days of hearing *Shammai's* say, 'Please can you give me 20-rupees fish?' The door of her house always remained closed. The only thing she glanced at every day through the tiny window was Kia's house. Abandoning her ritual of listening to Konkani songs on radio, she switched to cassettes playing devotional songs.

At around 10 in the morning, the bell rang on the road. It was the way to pass messages to the villagers that something had taken place or was going to take place. Whether good news or bad, the messenger announced it in detail. This was quicker than the newspaper, but it had limitations, as it was restricted only to a particular area. *Shammai* dashed to the door. She kept the cane at the corner of the doorpost. Placing both hands on the door, she put her ear next to the gap between the doors.

The man on the bicycle said, "Robert Vaz passed away. The funeral mass is at 4:30 in the evening, and the viewing of the body will be from 11 am onwards." It was heartbreaking news. He was the only oldest friend *Shammai* had in the village. For a moment, she forgot about Kia and thought about his death. She even considered going and confronting Gomes family and getting rid of her fear by confessing the truth. Simultaneously, she thought of her friend who would be in heaven and said in her mind, "If I go to Gomes' house, I will make things worse for myself." She held her steps and prayed for him being in her bedroom.

****

The Lobos' house was bombarded with questions about Kia's disappearance. Tina's answer was always the same—mouth shut, shaking her head rapidly from left to right. Though Tina got the shock of her life, she could not help the Gomes family with any information. She started her practice of lighting the candles at the Holy Cross, joining her hands, pleading for Kia's safe return. Her younger son had just got a new job on a cruise ship, so he was on a voyage. Her daughter-in-law, Jack's wife, was expecting and was at her mother's place. Tina was alone and feeling lonely. A doubt pricked Tina's heart constantly after Kia's disappearance. Having nobody to share with and seeking peace of mind, the more she suppressed it, the worse she became. She thought the best person to pour out her heart to was *Shammai.*

After the first letter from Toney, no more letters came. But in the last few years, she had received annual money from him. The sender's name was missing on the envelope, and Tina had no clue about it. She was sure it was *Shammai's* work, but she had no idea who was actually giving her the money. Although they were not on talking terms, they knew the other was of good heart. *Shammai* had just finished cooking rice and heating yesterday's curry for lunch. At about noon, there was a knock at her door. Every knock made her blood run cold. *Who might visit me at this hour? Is it the people from the Gomes family?* These and many more thoughts popped into her mind. Elbows pressed into her sides, making her body as small as possible, she peeped through the gap between the doors. And there she saw Tina—one handholding Christmas sweets and the other holding newspaper. Running her hands through her hair, she told herself, "Yes! It's a tradition to share Christmas sweets with the elderly and especially with families mourning their loved ones. I think today she is here just as an excuse to meet me." Tina knew *Shammai* had few teeth remaining and no sweet tooth. Heart to heart, she knew *Shammai* would be suspicious. Skin bunching around her eyes, with a pained stare, opened the door gently. She invited Tina into the house with a broad smile and accepted the sweets offered.

Tina fumbled for words and did not know what to say. Observing her lack of eye contact, *Shammai* said, "Why don't you sit?"

Tina, clearing her throat, sat on a hobbling antique chair. *Shammai* sat on a rocking chair. Both were in a stuffy, smelly sitting room. Both took a deep breath, and silence danced between them for a while. At a gut level, both had the same topic running through their minds. They felt uncomfortable speaking, since it had been years since they last talked. Breaking her knuckles, Tina broke the silence and said, "This is today's newspaper."

"What is special about it?" asked *Shammai* while taking the newspaper.

"Kia is still missing, and her coloured photo appeared today. Don't feel bad about me asking—do you have any idea about her?"

Shammai gazed at the photo and controlled her tears. She said hesitantly, "No, I know nothing about her."

"I had not told this to anyone, but I am telling you, for I trust you and I know you are good at heart. The other day, Kia met me behind her house in the woods. To my surprise, without concrete reason, she asked for my Toney's photo."

"You gave her Toney's photo?" *Shammai* stopped rocking the chair, hit her hand on her forehead, and continued, "I had hoped it would not happen." Biting her lips, she kept quiet.

With a small voice, Tina asked, "What's the matter?" *Shammai* cleared her throat and gripped her walking cane tightly. With a sad face, Tina said, "Okay, if you have nothing to say, I will make a move."

Shammai let her tears fall. Sniffing, she said, "I think I am responsible for all this. Kia accidentally landed in my compound on one occasion, and I spilled the beans about her father."

"Oh, I know now why she was in such a hurry to get the photo. She had plans to meet her daddy." Once again silence spread through the room.

Shammai took Tina to her bedroom. The holy pictures of saints were all over the lamp table. It appeared that all the saints were at work these days. The fresh flowers at the feet of the statue of Sacred Heart of Jesus showed he is the Lord of all the saints present in the room. Tina kissed the statue and said, "Lord, we trust you." *Shammai* walked towards the wooden cupboard and opened the heavy doors. She brought out a shirt and showed a tag. "This is the name of Toney's shop and the location."

"Oh *Shammai*, you knew everything about my son and you never told me."

"No, please don't misunderstand me. I tried to inform Jenny, but Rosemary did not give me a chance to speak. I got discouraged and kept everything to myself."

"Okay, never mind. Tell me—what you want to do now?"

With a blade, *Shammai* detached the tag and said, "This will help us find Toney"

Shammai led Tina to the kitchen where she reheated the leftover tea. Holding the teacups, they racked their brains on how to help Kia come home.

Squeak… squeak ... a noise came from behind the rice sacks. A mouse, wolfing the grains on full stomach, looked out from the big gap. *Shammai*, with trembling hands, missed the strike, and the mouse reversed. The fearful mouse scurried peacefully across the floor from the other side of the sack. The gape was small, yet safer.

Shammai furiously said, "Look at that tiny creature—escaped to the storeroom from the other side!"

Tina, with a smile on her face, said, "It knew not to go towards the danger."

Tina placed the empty teacup on the table. Pressing her lips, she said, "We too can apply his idea in our plan." *Shammai*, with crinkles on her forehead, asked, "What's running in your mind?"

Tina, coming closer, said, "We know it can be treacherous for us to go to the Gomes family to offer our help. We will find some other way. What do you say—if we go to Vasco to meet Toney? Though it may appear tough, yet it is a safer way,"

"Yeah, that sounds good, but how will you search for Kia?"

"Toney will know every nook and corner of Vasco, and he will help us look for his daughter." *Shammai* joined her hands and said, "I pray that what we have speculated may be true, and we may find our Kia"

Now things were falling into place for them, and they had joined enough dots. Tina grabbed *Shammai's* arm and said, "I don't think you will be able to travel with me by transit tomorrow."

Shammai turned her neck towards her arm and said, "I will do it, but I require a small favour from you."

"Definitely, I will help you."

"I had informed my grandson not to come for a few days. Immediately after this, please go to my grandson's place and tell him I want to talk to him right now."

"Why do you want him so urgently? Please don't involve him in the mess we created."

"Don't worry about him. He will be safe. Will you be here tomorrow morning at around 8:00 am?"

Both of them exchanged a smile. From the kitchen, Tina reached the main hall. *Shammai* said, "Now I know the purpose of your visit. You can take back the Christmas sweets."

Tina turned around and, winking her eye, said, "Your grandson will love to have them."

Chapter 17

Shop No 18

The morning of the 23rd of December was colder than what was predicted last night. Kia blocked her ears with a sponge to keep herself from catching a cold. She wanted to be back at Arun's house before the sun set, so she strode towards the south. Inhaling through the nose and releasing smoky breath from the mouth, she passed the railway station and walked along the tracks. The way was tricky, for it was not the regular path of the common folk.

The express train passed by, and the breeze blew Kia's hat a couple of meters away. The train didn't even honk at the station. She walked beside the tracks, suppressing the fear of passing trains. Her heart beat faster when she noticed a mother and a child crossing the railway track at a distance. If they had been thirty seconds earlier, the death of both would have been certain.

Kia walked for fifteen minutes. To avoid walking in the shrubs and bushes that spread along the path at the bottom of the tracks, Kia climbed the raised area that supported the rail. She felt a flutter in the pit of her stomach when she heard the train's horn. She sprinted on the slope of a jagged surface that supported the tracks. As she crossed the shrubbery, she stumbled on a stone and rolled down to the foot of the railroad. Her elbow and forehead were bruised after falling on the gray-black spiky stones. Applying her saliva to cool her wounds, she lifted the backpack and continued to walk in pain and agony. The ground she stood on was dirty. Alongside the railway line, passengers had strewn the area with plastic and papers. The waste became a blessing in disguise for Kia. An unopened packet of wafers and a half-filled water bottle energised the hungry Kia.

Partially refreshed, she turned right and passed through the passage leading to the city. Not a single person was on foot to speak to. All around, communication happened only through honking to wake up the drowsy drivers. The window shoppers had nothing to do with this area. The absence of petty shopkeepers, hawkers, and wanderers left the roads empty for the smooth running of vehicles. That made it even more difficult for Kia to inquire about the address.

Suddenly Kia gathered her courage and approached a labourer who was loading a truck. With a broad smile, she said, "Sir, can you help me figure out this address?"

"Sorry to tell you, I don't belong to this vicinity."

Kia's face dropped, "Thanks."

"Excuse me please—what happened to your forehead?"

"It's okay, forget about it."

"I think you need medication. Wait here, I will get the first aid box from the cabin." A harsh voice echoed from within the truck.

"What are you doing in the cabin? I employed you to load and not to drive, do your work." Kia heard the scolding and hid behind the electric pole at the edge of the wall, next to the main road.

"Boss, I came here in search of the first aid box."

"I don't see any bleeding on you. So what's wrong with you?"

"No boss, it's not for me. It's for the girl at the back." Boss glanced back and didn't find anyone.

"I don't see any person there."

"She must have sat on the road." The side mirror of the truck revealed the truth. The boss, with the euphonious tone, said, "Yes, I know where she is, though I doubt whether it's a he or she.

"You come out with the box and go continue your work. I will take care of that child."

Boss proceeded toward the pole and, with a silvery voice, said, "Leave the fear and the pole behind and come forward." Eyebrows squeezed together, hands almost curled into fists, she clung to the pole as she came forward. "Oh, you have a wound on your forehead. Come, let me apply the ointment," the boss said gently.

Kia loosened her muscles and released a deep breath. "Sir, I want another favour from you. Can you help me with this address?" With the sweat, the words had almost faded from the paper, and he struggled to read them. Kia knew it by heart.

She said, "It's Ashok road."

"Oh! Okay, to reach that area, go straight on this main road for about eighteen minutes. When you see a State Bank, take the road that goes to the right. After a five-minute walk, you will be in that area. But I don't know the exact location of the shop."

"Thanks a lot, sir, for the information. When I am in that area, I will ask someone for the shop name."

When she arrived at Ashok Road, Kia glanced at every shop's name board, peeped into the offices, and walked about for five to eight minutes. She saw the pleasing face of a middle-aged woman in a colourful shop. It was the only outstanding, well-designed office on the street. Kia caught the bag's straps tight and stepped into the office. With a pleasant smile, like that of a good saleswoman, the woman behind the desk said, "Yes, what brings you here? Do you want to place an order for party bags?" As Kia walked closer, noticing the white antiseptic powder on her wounds, the woman said, "Oh sorry—this is not a nursing home or dispensary. If you take five hundred steps from here, you will find the convent of Missionaries of Charity sisters. They will surely treat your wounds and may give you a place to lay your head for a night. Why don't you go there?"

Kia, dropping her chin to her chest and pressing her lips, said, "Yes, I feel small. At the same time, I am lost in this sparsely populated place." Kia's humility won the heart of that woman.

She said with a caring voice, "Were you sent here by your parents to purchase fancy items, and something happened, and then you lost everything? Am I right?"

Kia loosened her hands and kept them on the desk. "No, don't consider me your customer. I want a favour from you. I want you to guide me to this address."

"Oh, It's 'Kia the tailors'"

"Yes, you know where it's located?"

"Yes! Definitely, it is right at the corner—Shop no.18."

Kia clasped her hands to her chest and exclaimed, "Really! I am so close to it. Thank God, and thank you."

The woman said, "Hey, wait please! Why are you jumping for joy? What's the matter?"

Kia sighed, and the tears of happiness rolled down her cheeks. She said, "I am meeting my daddy after many years."

"Oh, so nice. I am happy for you. Have a great day—hurry up and don't waste time."

Kia leaped down the steps of the office to the road. Because of the ripple of excitement, she dodged death between the speeding cars. At a distance of a few meters, she noticed her name on the front board. Gazing at it, she beamed from ear to ear and felt light in her chest. She rushed to the shop; unfortunately, the railroad gravel marred her sandals and compelled her to walk barefoot. Grabbing them in her hand, she dashed through the door.

A man at the sewing machine stared at her—not through, but above his soda-glass spectacles. Kia exclaimed, "Daddy!" Her hands dropped on realizing he was an elderly person.

"I'm Widower, without kids," he said with his mouth open.

"I am sorry! Please, can you tell me where Toney is?"

"Who is Toney? There is no one by that name here."

"No, that's not true. This is his shop, and he named it after his daughter." The man scratched his head and got up from the chair, for Kia's words had thrown him off balance.

"My dear child, I don't understand what you are trying to say." Kia contracted her forehead, paused for a while, and then brought out the photo. "Okay, then you will surely know this man."

The man took the photo. "No, my dear, I don't know him."

"No, if he is not the owner, then he may be an employee here."

Handing the photo back, he said, "Sorry, no one with a beard works here." She realised that it was her mistake to draw a beard in the photo. Kia's face turned dull.

She said, "Please see it once again and confirm, because he is my daddy."

"To tell you frankly, most of us here are Hindus and clean-shaven, and the owner is Suraj. He is a bachelor"

"Are there any Christians who own a tailoring shop here?"

"No! As per my knowledge, there are a handful of Christians in the next lane, and none of them are tailors by profession. Mostly, they run medical stores or bars." She covered her eyes with her palm, leaned back on the doorpost, sank to her knees, and began crying.

The man bent down, came to her level, laid his hand on her back, and consoled her, "Dear child, I don't know who you are searching for, but I'm sure that you are longing to meet someone who is very dear to you." Kia, wiping her tears, stood up. He said, "Daughter, now you go back home. Your people must be in search of you." These words reminded Kia of losing her way back the previous day. Her efforts were in vain. She gave upon her quest for her daddy.

She moved the bill of her hat to the side and grabbed her bag by the handle. She came out of the shop, turned, and had a last look at her name on the shop, with the slack expression wet, dull eyes. Then, on the heavy feet, she walked away. Her neck bent, face pointed towards the road, she moved to the road.

At a distance on the road, there was a mirage. On her bare feet, she chased it. She couldn't stay in one spot for long. The unbearable heat of the tarred road intensified her tears and thirst. The wrapped layer of plastic bag protected her feet, making her chase a bit better. The railway gravel was harsh on her, tearing apart the plastic and her fragile feet.

In severe pain, she left footprints dipped in blood on the floor of the railway station. Without looking into the eyes of the passengers, she walked straight towards a corner where a cobbler sat and said, "Sir, please stitch my sandals. I am short of money. I have only this precious thing to pay you."

Holding the back screw of her earring, the avaricious cobbler said, "This will not work. And what I will do with this? It will cost you the whole earring."

Kia was pushed up against the wall, and with a heart-rending tone she said, "Okay, take this, but be fast." Abruptly abandoning with what he was busy, he poked Kia's sandal with the needle.

Not wanting to waste time, Kia took the opportunity and walked towards the toilets. Though the queue at the men's toilet was longer than the women's, it was moving faster. Kia was in two minds about which line to join. She tightened her fist, took a deep breath, and accepted the reality of her gender. In the queue, she got to stay in third place. In a minute, a group of young teenagers came and stood in the line. All were well-dressed. Their beauty was easy on the eyes of all the men in the opposite queue. Kia felt like a fish out of water. Pulling down her T-shirts hem, with a downward gaze, she stood still.

The afternoon sweeper lady walked between the male and the female line. She turned towards the females and requested them to move a bit to sweep. They gave the deaf ear to the sweeper woman. Kia smiled at that slim lady and promptly moved to the side. She giggled while the sweeper snaked the broom between their legs. They gave a pained look to Kia.

One among them said, "Don't go closer to that oafish girl front of you. It looks to me she hasn't taken a shower for days."

The other said, "I doubt she is a girl, and it's so surprising that she has a summer cut in the winter. Ahaha!"All chuckled, keeping their hands over their mouths.

"Oh, did you notice her ear? Only one earring is dangling," said the last one.

Kia inhaling deeply through her nose, then exhaling through her mouth, thought to herself, *'Why I should lose my peace? I am a female and I am in the female toilet. I am proud to be who I am.'* Kia made up her mind and left behind all fears of being a girl.

The sweeper lady overheard their conversation between the teenagers. She said, "My dear youngsters, to tell you the truth, she has natural beauty. In your case, you felt you are not beautiful enough. That's why you feel the need for makeup. As compared to yours, she has a million-dollar smile. All this will pass away another day. These days we speak about gender equality. First, we have to learn to respect other females; then only can we expect men to respect us."

With a slow smile that broke across their faces, they said, "Yes, we are sorry." Kia thanked the sweeper lady and rushed inside the washroom, before someone else took her place.

She returned just as the cobbler finished the last stitch. Moments later, Kia—still wearing only one earring—walked out of the station.

That afternoon, Shop No. 18 was polished with truth as the owner poured out his heart.

"Today, late morning, a tomboy visited the shop and asked for a Toney," said Sabu.

"What! A girl was searching for me?" Suraj said.

"I did not say she was looking for you," Sabu said.

To divert the attention, Suraj said, "Oh, okay, hmmm, maybe someone else in the locality."

"Though she said that Toney owns this shop, and I am sure it's not you. She called him daddy."

"Wait a minute," he grabbed a newspaper and said, "Is this her?"

"Yes, she was wearing a hat and had very short hair, but with a bangle and earrings. If not for that, anyone would have mistaken her for a boy."

Suraj spilled his guts. "Uncle Sabu, yes, she is my daughter, but the paper says that she is missing."

"What! You are married and have a daughter?"

"Yes! I am not Suraj, I am Toney. I am very sorry for being with you for years and keeping you in the dark." Toney broke down and cried. He banged his head on the door and said, "Oh uncle, what did you tell her, and which side did she walk to?"

"I told her there is no one here called Toney, and then she wept and walked to the right."

"Oh my Kia, where are you, and where shall I find you? Sabu uncle, I am going to file a complaint at the police station."

"That you can do tomorrow. Now go to the place and search. After all, she is on her feet and must have not gone far."

Chapter 18

Pervert Eyes

Kia stepped out from the railway station into the noon sunlight. Her eyes hunted for the familiar roads. The road with potholes on the side of the playground was the same road she had walked last night. Sticking to the two-meter boundary wall of the ground, she proceeded.

Just a stone's throw away, the noise of cheering and screaming from the playground reached Kia. She heard the words of one who said, "Yes, it's a six, and we need 10 more runs to win." She ignored the clamour of the batting cricket team after losing a proficient wicket. They all sat on the cement benches under the mango tree and calculated the runs to win. The spectators and the players had their eyes wide open and applauded the batsman.

Kia approached closer to the corner of the playground. One cricketer whistled at Kia to grab her attention. Unfortunately, it did not work. However, it made others aware of Kia's presence. Someone with a deliberate cough said, "Hi! Tomboy, nice to have you in our avenue, with one earring and a bangle. I can not only give you earrings, but rings for the nose and for the index toe. Hahahaha."

"Hey, I don't think she is Hindu. The way she is dressed has the answer. She belongs to my faith. I am the right one to give her a wedding ring," said the boy who had worn a chain with a big cross. Very mischievous, one of them purposely dropped the ball in front of Kia and said, "Hey, you, my dear, please throw the ball back to me."

Kia tightened her fist and strode without even glancing at the open gutters along the sidewalk. When the ball had bounced before her and had reached her leg, she kicked it into the gutter and gave a stern message to everyone present there. She was alone and was a new face, so she became the target for eve-teasing. Though she was confident and content to be a girl, those terrifying thoughts about Vasco were still fresh in her mind.

The shouting and howling lingered only in the middle of the playing field. At the corner, the teammates and supporters had shut their mouths. The calmness among them teased their minds and hurt their ego. The thoughts of teaching her a lesson popped into their minds. One thought of throwing a bat at her. He even ran with the bat to the edge of the playground and leaned on the 3-foot wall.

Kia pretended to walk towards the police station, just opposite the main road. The boy who had teased her froze, and like a dog sticking his tail between its legs, came back. Kia crossed the road, turned back, and stared at those boys. Pointing at the police station, she had warned them. The boys, out of fear, joined their hands and asked for pardon. With joy within, she smiled and felt proud of her act.

The ground on which Kia stood had private buses parked as the boundary wall. Every bus conductor called out the names of the places which they were scheduled to take passengers. Kia's ears did not hear the name of her destination. The easiest way to arrive at the location she was familiar with was to inquire about the direction to the popular museum. Drivers were the best people to start with for the inquiry. The answer which she got was, "You are not in the wrong place. It's right behind that mega building."

It was Saturday. It was a day assigned for a half-day's work. The museum had more public gatherings to make the maximum use of their Christmas holidays. Most of the hawkers and vendors had already called it a day. The only person she saw next to the door of the museum was the watchman. She took Leader's chew and mourned over the death of Leader. Though she was not in a black outfit, she was next to the black dustbin. The late afternoon daylight assisted her in tracing back the way she pursued Leader from the laundry shop.

Freaking hungry, Kia at last reached a familiar lane leading to her destination. With a stooped face, she trudged on the mud road. The day light was losing its brightness, and folks were pacing back home. The air pushed the aroma of evening food from the homes. Tiny houses smiled with lighted bulbs and candles through their windows and doors. Some children, empty-handed, sat at the doorsteps expecting sweets from their fathers when he came back from work. The evening breeze was out to have fun at night. Kia put out her peach-colored scarf with pink flowers and rolled it around her neck gallantly.

The narrow lane leading to Arun's house was around the corner. Kia's heart was becoming lighter at the same time. She was anxious about Arun's reaction of knowing the truth about her gender. She hoped for the better. After all, it was only a one-night stay. What to tell her family was another concern running through her mind. However, she knew her greatest source of security at home was Mr. Gomes; he had defended her from scolding on many occasions.

The aroma of fried chicken knocked at her nostrils. Pramod sat at the food joint and enjoyed crispy chicken. The bulb at the stall just switched on, and the flies had begun gathering around it. A few flies fell into Pramod's plate; however, he was least bothered. His greedy eyes had been hunting Kia since last night. The fast-food center was right at the corner of the narrow lane to his house. Yesterday and today, he put his tongue out like a dog, waiting for Kia. After a long time, he had stayed sober for two days.

His heart jumped with joy at seeing her, and he came out, as if wagging his tail in excitement. When he approached Kia, he said, "Oh, Karthik, where were you yesterday? We searched for you in every possible place. Hope you were at the safe place."

Kia felt a bit comforted. She halted, placed her bag down, and said, "I am okay, I just missed the way back."

"Oh, it is obvious in the crowded vicinity. What about Leader? Where is he?"

Stuttering, with a soft voice, she said, "I lost him. While I was sleeping last night at the bus stand, he went missing. I don't know who took him." She told him lies so that he wouldn't ask further questions. She then said, "I am famished."

Pramod, tipping the head to the side, said "I see an earring, necklace, and a bangle."

"Oh! I am very sorry that I told everyone the lie. The truth is, I am a girl. I wanted to save myself with evil eyes."

Pramod was happy and was in seventh heaven. He said, "Oh, that's intelligent of you, but now what made you change your mind?"

Kia raised her eyebrows and said, "Well, I guess it's time to face the challenges of being a girl." He thought this piece of information was like a cherry on the cake for his plan. Before he could ask her more questions, Kia said, "Let's go home to eat." He replied immediately, "Do you like fried rice?"

"Yes," she said, without giving it a second thought.

"Come, follow me," he said, taking his steps in the opposite direction of the house.

Kia said, "I am okay without fried rice. I will manage whatever is available at home."

"No, no, I want to give you a treat today. Today is like Independence Day for you. And even if we go home, there won't be any food left. What we had in the afternoon was yesterday's remaining food." Kia bowed her head and walked behind him.

The evening grew older, but the distance to the food count was getting longer. The breeze, loaded with a variety of aromas, tempted young and old to eat at the streets corners. They ignored ordinary food stalls to reach the best one in the slum. Kia, dead tired, could not keep up with him, so she requested, "Uncle, will you do the purchase and meet me here at this public tap?"

"No, dear, I want you to join me in that lovely place. You will get to enjoy hot fried rice. If you're tired, give your bag to me, and you will feel light. It's just half a kilometre away from here."

Kia loosened her shoulders, landing her hands on her waist. She said, "Okay, let me drink some water first."

Every step led them to the abated noise of shutting doors due to the growing darkness. It was 7 pm; the clanger of the church bell at the Anglos confirmed it. Their journey continued through the outskirts of the slums, and they left all the food joints behind.

Now the darkness was darker. In the absence of street and house lights, Kia asked ten times, "Where have we reached, and how much time to reach the restaurant?" To that, she got the same answer, "Will you have some patience? We are getting close."

At last, Pramod halted in a dark, mysterious fenced compound wall. Kia was freezing in the cold breezy late evening. She could perceive only shadows around her, created by the workshop's 60-watt bulb. Pramod knocked at the door. The change in his tone and language had more holes than Swiss cheese. Kia realised something was fishy. She quietly moved her leg aside and prepared to run. At that very moment, Pramod grabbed her hand. She shouted, "Help! Help! Help!"

By then, her voice reached the ears of the watchmen of the neighbourhood industry. A man from inside pushed a cloth in her mouth. With great effort, he dragged Kia inside. The dark, tall man biting his lips stared at Kia and said, "Hey, you! I don't want to hear any noise and see any movements." Keeping his finger on his mouth with a strong voice, he said, "Shut your mouth." Head flinching back slightly and eyebrows squished together, he turned to Pramod and said, "Are you sure you have brought the right child?" Holding his hands loosely behind his back, he said, "Don't worry. Though she looks like a tomboy, she is worth millions." The dark man tied Kia to a pole. Kia sobbed. Pramod said, "Keep her safe tonight. I shall come tomorrow night to make the delivery."

Chapter 19

The Waltz

They set the inquiry table in a four-walled room with no window, to prevent peeping outside and to reduce the torture of investigation. The golden light was reflected in his tears, and he trembled in the presence of a man in Khaki. "Tell us where you have hidden her and what you expect in return," said the police inspector, with a gruff voice.

"No, I don't know where she is, and how could a father kidnap his own daughter," Toney said with a feeble voice.

"Her family members have held you responsible for her disappearance. What do you say about it?"

Toney, with quivering hands, palm facing the officer, said, "No, no, they just want to take revenge on me. Yes! Because I left Jenny alone years back."

Toney's words, spoken without hesitation and the genuineness on his face, made the inspector calm down, and he said, "Anyhow, you have to be in our custody until we find the child."

Toney hit his hands on his forehead, pulled his hair, and said, "Oh no, please listen to me."

The police constable who had arrested Toney while he had come to lodge a complaint of the missing girl said, "Sir, I think we need to listen to him too. Let's give him a chance."

The inspector's voice mellowed, "Hey, you, tell us the truth."

"Yesterday, in my absence, Kia came to my shop. It seems she had shortened her hair, and anyone would have mistaken her for a boy."

"Don't share cooked stories and waste my time."

"Please trust me. I am telling the truth. Otherwise, call and ask my assistant, Sabu."

"Then what happened?"

"Sabu was not aware of my past. So, he informed her that no one by the name Toney was at the shop."

"Then where did she go? Do you have any information on where she stayed these past days?"

Toney pointed toward the south and said, "Sabu mentioned to me that after talking to her, she didn't seem like the daughter of an entrepreneur. But she told him, 'I was not born in a slum, but my decisions led me there.' That's why I came here to ask you to search for her in the slums."

The inspector took off his hat and said, "I hope you are telling the truth."

The Gomes family and their relatives reached Vasco midmorning. It was Christmas Eve, and a Sunday. The family thought it would be easy to drive around the city their first visit was to the museum. At the gate, when Rita let Leader down, he darted towards Jenny.

When they realised it wasn't the city but the slums, they were compelled to leave the car and had to walk. From the large, well-populated Vasco city, they changed their direction to the slums.

The morning grew into noon. Keeping their eyes peeled, they all looked for the girl who appeared like a tomboy.

Jenny's eyes welled with tears at the sight of the shabby, tone clothes of children on the muddy streets of the slum. The walk between the tiny houses melted their hearts. Mr. Gomes felt uneasy amidst the buzzing sound of flies in the latrines. Being a diabetic, he had no choice but to catch his nose and ease himself. Claustrophobic Rosemary complained all the way and blamed Toney for hiding Kia in the narrow lanes. Toney, like a mad dog, approached everyone and inquired about any unfamiliar girl of 13 years old. Some slum dwellers thought that he was the criminal surrounded by police, and others thought that he was the police officer in mufti. Police swept almost the entire area with sirens and announcements, but no one could identify the photo. All the efforts were going in vain as time flew, and in the blue sky, cranes flew back home before nightfall.

The Gomes' family assembled at the intersection, discouraged. At the suggested place, the police jeep came and halted. A man in a blue shirt came out, followed by police. At first glance, Jenny failed to recognize him. When she looked into his eyes, she darted forward and grabbed his collar. She shouted at the top of her voice, "You have taken my daughter! What wrong have I done to you? Why can't you see me happy?"

Toney pushed her hands off and said, "Hey, please control yourself. Don't blame me for your negligence. You couldn't take care of my child."

Jenny widened her eyes and tightened her fist, saying, "What are you saying? You are the one who left your little daughter and escaped reality?"

Nodding his head, Toney said, "Yes, I had not come back, and when I tried to contact you to explain the reason, you did not even bother to get in touch with me. You immediately saw another man and forgot about me. The pain you caused me, I will never forget." The heated argument was lacking abusive words before until the inspector and Mr. Gomes took away Toney. "Hey you! Now you are blaming me, you irresponsible man! I will never forgive you."

Toney, biting his nails and turning his neck now and then, tried to tell them he was innocent in the police vehicle. Mr. Gomes, who had hauled Toney to the vehicle, caught his ear and said, "You rouge! Don't speak without evidence. My daughter always loved you more than anyone else. And for your kind information, she did not remarry." Toney, with his mouth wide open, cried bitterly and recalled all he had said to Jenny. Mr. Gomes went closer to the inspector, opened his wallet, and then placed his hand into the inspector's hand, saying, "Keep that monster in prison until we find Kia." The Gomes family had clustered around the cars.

Jenny caressed Leader tightly, talking to him while still sobbing, "Do you know where Kia is? I wish you could talk," she let Leader on the ground.

"Oh, that reminds me of the last option—use a sniffer dog. If you have any things that belongs to Kia, please keep them ready. We will call for one or two sniffers." Mr. Gomes rushed to the car, opened the trunk, dragged out the backpack with clothes, and threw the playing items out in a hurry to fetch the clothes. As a result, Kia's favourite flying disc landed at a meter's distance close to Leader. He sniffed it, caught it by the jaw, and ran off. Leader jumped over the potholes, not minding the paws dipping in the cow dung. The aroma of fried samosas and spilled food from the garbage bin could not distract him.

One of Jenny's young cousins ran after him and was about to step on the leash. Jenny screamed, "Please don't stop, just follow." Her cousin halted. Jenny turned back, waved her hands, and exclaimed, "Hey! All of you, please come. We are definitely close to Kia."

The young cousin asked her, "How can you say so confidently?"

She caught him by his hand, continuing to jog, and keeping an eye on Leader.

In the darkness, with her eyes covered, Kia was lost. All day long, the bang of a hammer to remove the dent from a car deafened her. She opened her fingers to feel the clue that gestured toward her surroundings, communicating with grease and nut bolts. The cloth tied over her mouth absorbed her saliva. Tiny ants grazed on the morning's fallen, dried tea, and as they marched back to their nest, they crossed over Kia's legs. She could feel them but couldn't see where they were. She tried to shake them off, but they crawled into her clothes. Every bite left her skin red.

She had lost track of time, but heard the *azaan* and she realised it was the time for *Namaz.* She guessed it must be 6:30 in the evening. Immediately after that, she could feel the robust, hard biceps of hands lifting her. In the other place, there was a soft seat, but felt suffocated. At the bang of the door, she heard a squeak from a woman at the corner. Outside, she heard a shrill voice: "I think we should give them something to eat before we transport them."

A bass voice replied, "I had given them tea and bread in the morning; that's enough."

"No, we have to give them some fruits and water. If they faint and are found unconscious the following morning, they will not have much worth."

"Okay, fine. I will fetch something to eat."

Kia was inquisitive to know who was with her at the new place. She tapped her feet and expected a reply from inside. Then she tapped it rhythmically. Two more pairs of feet kept the same tempo. She understood there were more people trapped with her. Others locked inside the doors were shivering. Their sweat drenched their clothes. No words, no sign language to communicate any message to others. Only ears could converse and comfort each other. Kia constantly made some noise with feet to pass the message to others that they were not alone.

Leader scratched the doors of a van parked outside the garage gate. Wagging his tail, he waited to open the door and hand over the disc to Kia. A few seconds later, the younger cousin arrived and said, "Hey, Leader, why did you run if you had to stay at this van? You made us tired for no reason." Leader took rounds of the van, still holding the disc in his firm bite. Panting for breath, the other cousin reached, bowing from the waist. She said, "Where is Leader, and why did you halt here?"

"Leader is at the front of the van. I don't know why he has stopped suddenly."In a couple of minutes, Jenny, walking briskly, reached the location. Keeping her finger on her lips, Jenny said, "Please keep quiet! Shh... listen." The sound of tapping of feet grew louder. The cousins called out Kia by her name. Now, the tapping was much louder. Jenny knew Kia's talent for dance. She played a waltz bit with her wrist and fingers on the side of the van. The replies emerged from inside: one bit played with the heel and two bits on the toes. She looked up, smiled wholeheartedly, palm on her mouth, and tears of happiness streamed down her weary cheeks. She took the phone and called her father and the police inspector.

A man balancing water bottles in his armpit and bread in his arms came closer to the van. Narrowing his eyes, squinting around the van, he said, "What are you guys doing here, next to my van? Go away from here." As he turned towards Leader, Jenny's finger on her lips, signalled her cousins. He left the bread on the top of the van, pointing his finger, he said, "Before I call my friends, go away. And while going back, take this creature with the toy too." They took their steps back as if they were moving away without uttering a word. He opened the cabin, left the·items he bought on the seat, and called his partner over the phone.

Jenny messaged, 'Hurry before we lose them'. Leader still lingered around the van. He came out and kicked Leader to chase him away. Jenny turned back and said, "Leader, come back."

Leader, still holding the disc, showed his disagreement. The second man roughly opened the gate. Widening his eyes, he pretended as if he was clearing the leaves and the milk of the Jackfruit tree, which had overshadowed the van. He pointed the dagger at his companion and said, "Go get in, we have to reach by night"

On noticing the red car, Jenny gained courage. Walking with wide steps towards them, she said, "Hey, what is in the van?"

The man, spitting forcefully, pointed the dagger at her, pulling his sleeves, and said, "It is none of your business. Get away from here."As he took steps towards Jenny, a red car halted next to them. From the car, the inspector said, "Hands up and be on your knees."

"Dear, where is Kia?" said Mr. Gomes. Jenny kept her hand on her mouth and pointed to the door.

"Hey, you, come and open the door," said the inspector.

"No, no. Sir, there is no one there; we are transporting spare parts for vehicles." Knock after knock was heard from inside.

"Are you taking live spare parts? I don't want more explanation. Open it now." The man turned red. With a trembling hand, he opened the door. Leader jumped in, kept the disc at Kia's feet, and licked her from bottom to top. All tied up, Kia just attempted to rub her body against him. Both the criminals joined their hands, begging for mercy, blaming someone else.

The inspector released Kia from the bondage. She darted to her mother, hugging her tightly. The tears of happiness rolled down from their eyes. For a while, only silence prevailed. The inspector arrested the human trafficker sand took the other two girls into police custody. Jenny caressed and kissed Kia many times. Leader nuzzled both mother and daughter and wagged his tail.

"Darling, how are you?" Jenny said while searching for any wounds or scars on her body.

"I am fine, mother."

Jenny wiped Kia's tears and said, "Do you know how much I missed you? At one point, I thought I had lost you forever."

Kia bent a little and kissed the cheek of her kneeling mother, saying, "Yes, mamma, I missed you too."

Jenny, still thinking that Toney had taken Kia, said, "My sweetheart, I know that man is not good."

"Yes, mamma, he told me a lie and brought me here yesterday evening," Kia replied, thinking of Pramod.

Jenny looked at Kia with compassionate eyes and, with a gentle smile, said, "Now don't worry. I am with you, and he is with the police."

"But I don't understand how his son is good, and he is so greedy." Kia pondered aloud.

Hand flying on her chest, Jenny said, "What! He has a son?" Jenny could not control her tears; she wiped her eyes. She thought that Toney had remarried after their separation.

"Mother, what are you thinking? Why do you look sad?" Kia kissed Jenny on her cheek again and said, "Don't be disheartened. Now I am with you." Jenny smiled at her beloved daughter.

By then, all the others arrived at the site, all excited. Everyone wanted to hear Kia's story, and they bombarded her with questions. Kia was famished, and her face was drooping. Jenny intervened and requested everyone to go back home, saying, "Thanks to all! We shall meet tomorrow evening for a party, and then you can ask as many questions as you have for Kia."

Jenny and Kia got in Mr. Gomes' car and went to the police station. On the way, Jenny fed her beef tongue roast in bread. Kia devoured it, gulping it down with water. The rest of the relatives, along with Rosemary, hit the road back home.

Chapter 20

Under the Mistletoe

The cold evening, dressed in lights and adorned with colourful decorations, brought the message: God loved the world, so He gave it to His only son. Caroling on the city streets, party spirit in the air filled the hearts of all who longed for the birth of the Lord Jesus. Kia was fast asleep on her mother's lap in the car. A dreadful day had exhausted her. Though the distance was short, the tragic accident on the road made it feel longer.

Jenny rested her cheek on her palm and stared outside through the car window. Though shadows of tall buildings passed by the car, not a single one disturbed her. Mr. Gomes, at the steering, yawned. Clearing his eyes, he said, "Jenny," but no reply came from the back seat. "Jenny, Jenny, are you there?"

Jenny swung her head, blinked her eyes, raised her eyebrows and said, "What Papa! Have we reached the police station?"

"No, my dear, I just wanted to ask you how you feel now."

"Papa, today my heart is torn into pieces. And I don't know what to do."

"What are you saying? Today I expected you to be happy. Kia is back."

"Papa, I know I should be happy today. I am sad because he is married and even has a child. Was leaving not enough?"

Mr. Gomes stretched his hand back, touched her head, and said, "Sweetheart, you are not alone in your pain. We all are with you."

She sniffed and responded, "Yes, Papa, this time I will not deny your choice."

Now, the silence was so profound that Kia's heavy breathing could be heard. The car slowed down and stopped with a brake in front of the police station. He shook Jenny's shoulders; upon waking, she asked, "Have we reached?"

"Yes, come out, and let Kia be there in the car."

"No, no. I don't want us to be apart."

She tied her hair, gave her bag to Mr. Gomes, and lifted Kia in her arms, walking straight to the bench next to the lockup. She placed Kia on the bench near the bars.

"Jenny, oh My Jenny, forgive me please for accusing you of remarriage."

A voice cried for mercy, emerging from behind the bars in the cell. Jenny paid it no attention, speeding up to the desk. She said, "Sir, we are in a hurry. Please give me the complaint draft to sign."

The voice became louder. A constable on night duty said, "Hey, you! Please maintain silence. It's past 10 pm; others are getting disturbed."

"No, sir, please give me a chance to speak to Jenny. I just want to apologise."

"No one is here to visit you, and we don't allow anyone to meet at this time."

"Sir, she is my wife."

"Has she told us that you are her husband? No, right?"

Toney gripped the bars, bowed his head, and went on his knees.

Kia got up with a start. She turned her head all around, finding herself in an unfamiliar place. She cried out, "Mother, where you are?" Those cries of Kia breathed life into Toney. He said, "Kia, my daughter, I love you. Look at your right; I am here."

Jenny shouted, "Kia, don't talk to strangers."

Kia was stunned.

"Mother, that's my daddy, Toney!"

"Kia, now don't act as if you know nothing."

"No, mother, I don't know him."

"Are you sure?"

"Yes!"

"Then who is that person who kidnapped you?"

"The person with scars on his face at the van's location—he is Arun's daddy, Pramod."

Jenny was shocked.

"Mother, I actually came to Vasco to find my daddy."

"What! You came to search for him?"

Kia nodded, sprinted towards Toney, and extended her hands toward him. They touched each other's heads and cried.

Jenny said, "Kia, leave him and come here."

"No mother, he is my father, and you don't know how much he loves you."

"Kia, stop talking like a grown up. You are still a girl and ignorant of the truth."

"Mother, I know the truth; *Shammai* told me the entire story."

Jenny pressed her lips, caught Kia's shoulder, and said, "Enough of your lies! Come with me."

Kia went on her knees, joined her hands as if in a prayer.

"Mother! My daddy never intended to leave you alone. He still is alone. Mother, he wrote you letters, but you didn't reply."

"I know he wrote me a few letters."

"No, mother, you are mistaken. It is not only two letters, but letters upon letters. Initially, he thought the letters took time to arrive, so he called you over the phone. You did not receive his calls and never replied to any of the letters. Now tell me, mother, who is at fault?"

Jenny had no words, and there was a pin-drop silence for a while.

"Jenny, whatever the child has said is right. I am really sorry for hurting you last night. Your father told the truth to me," Toney said with his hands joined.

"Mother, forgive him please, and let us start a new life as a family," said Kia.

Heartbroken, Jenny was not in the position to forgive him. The half-opened door let the chilled breeze in. The night grew colder. Fans switched off, and the door closed. There was a request for blankets, heard from behind the bars.

Jenny's father intervened. He now understood how the two people in love had been deliberately kept apart—and that their union would bring them a lifetime of happiness.

"My dear child, I listened to whatever you said. On hearing your words, I think Toney deserves to be released." Facing Jenny, he said, "It is a blessing to have such a husband, who toiled to bring a smile to your face. I understand he has hurt you, and it is painful to forgive. I don't want to say forgive him for the sake of your daughter. It will not be a genuine forgiveness. Forgive him from the depth of your heart. It is not only his fault. If you can forgive your mama, who lied to you, then why can't you forgive the person who loved you and worked day and night, hoping that one day you would come back? If he wanted, he could have enjoyed life after leaving you—but no, he didn't do that. To forgive him is like piercing a needle, but unless a needle is pierced, we can't stitch the clothes. Kia has pained both of you by leaving the house. You both went in search of her. She was like a needle that pierced you both, causing pain, yet her purpose was to join you together. For without pain, nothing can truly be bound. Jenny, let not the efforts of your daughter go in vain."

As Jenny was calming down, she saw two ladies at the doorpost of the police station. Looking at the wrinkled face, she said,

"Oh, you all are a part of this drama. And you, *Shammai*! What brings you here so late at night? That means you knew where my daughter was all these days. You are the best at hiding people. We can't trust anyone here."

Jenny cried from her heart and continued,

"Why me, Lord? They don't even understand what is going on within me."

"Mother, what are you saying? Why are you blaming *Shammai* for my mistake?" Kia asked.

"Kia, you are young and you know nothing about her, and you mentioned just before that she told you everything. That is why you left us and came in search of him. Now tell me, who should be held responsible?"

Kia reluctantly said, "No, Mother! Please listen to us."

"Will you give me a chance to speak?" Coming forward, *Shammai* said.

Mr. Gomes kept his hand on Jenny's shoulder and said, "Dear, let us listen to what she has to say."

Shammai went near the entrance table, leaning on it. She said, "Yes, I am responsible, and I was the one who instigated Kia. Yes, I was selfish, because if I didn't reunite you, I would not be with my husband in heaven. Jenny! Do you remember when you were staying in Seachol? You asked me why they had hidden idols of Hindu Gods in the house. And I diverted your mind by saying that they had given the house to Hindus for rent. It was all a lie. By birth, my husband was a staunch Hindu, born in a Brahmin family. I know the power of love. Although it was difficult to fall in love in our days, since society moved according to the norms of arranged marriage, my beloved husband broke all barriers to win my love. It was my father who had placed a condition before him. 'You convert to Christianity or leave her hand.' He sacrificed everything for me and became Peter from Prabudesi. He got baptised and embraced Jesus.

When I got to know your love story, I made up my mind to help you at any cost. I did not know that it would backfire. It was vivid in your eyes, the love for each other. I knew the taste of love. So I thought your love would last like ours. Who knew that love is not always the same in all cases? I had no bad intentions. Yes, I admit it was my mistake. I thought this amazing kid would bring some change. But I accept that she didn't do things the way I wished—she did them in her own way. Now I don't know how to thank her for the great courage she showed, despite being a girl.

Jenny, I am not here to blame you. I am here to blame me for my imprudent act. I only know how much Toney loved you when he left you. He is still burning in your love. What he told me when he was at Vasco, he has kept his promise. He promised not to remarry and wait for you till his death. He worked hard all these years so that you may have a better life when he comes back. The last thing I want you to think about is, from on your part, have you at ever attempted to search for him and learn about his side of the story? Sorry to say, your mother blinded you. And by the way, we came to bailout Toney and did not know that you too are here."

Mr. Gomes said to Jenny, "Dear, I think it's time for you to forgive him." Jenny placed her head on Mr. Gomes' shoulders and sobbed. The inspector opened the lockup, bowing respectfully. Toney stepped forward, chest tight with relief. Seeing Kia, gratitude and love flooded him. "I love you, Kia, and thank you for taking a risk for my sake," he said, his voice trembling.

Kia wiped her tears, hope and worry in her eyes, and whispered, "Dada, you have to promise me you will take me to the Solva spring."

Toney smiled, eyes glistening with tenderness. "Sure, my sweetheart," he said, holding her hand warmly, silently promising care and protection.

Toney said to Jenny with a soft tone, "Jenny, I have always loved you more than myself. I know you must still be wondering why I left you—and that too, on the birthday of our child. It was my fault… my greatest mistake. I failed to tell you the truth. Yes, in real love, nothing should be hidden. But I was weak, afraid—afraid to say 'no' to you, afraid to disappoint you in any way. Whenever you asked for something, I gave in, even when I couldn't afford it. I borrowed money from friends, piling up debts, yet I kept pretending everything was fine. I thought love meant protecting you from worries, carrying the weight alone.

Now I understand… true love is not about hiding pain or pretending to be strong. It's about being honest, being transparent, and carrying our crosses together. I failed you, Jenny. I failed to share my burden with you. And now, after all these years, I know in my heart—you would never have left me, even if I was struggling. You proved it by staying faithful, by choosing to remain single all this time. That truth breaks me and heals me at the same time. Thank you, my love, for your faithfulness. Please… forgive me. I promise you, Jenny—I will never leave you alone again." He wiped his tears onto his shoulders and stood silent.

Jenny, leaving her dad's shoulder, darted towards him and strike him on his chest, saying, "It's Christmas night. Meet me behind the cemetery to apologize." He embraced her tightly. The clock rang. It was 12:00 a.m., the time for midnight Christmas mass. For Kia, it was a Christmas miracle. Everyone around them applauded.

One among them said, "Live long, your love."

Another prisoner said, "Sir, please give me your phone. I want to say sorry to my wife on this Christmas day."

The police station was filled with love and forgiveness. Their kiss under the mistletoe brought tears to all the witnesses.

Jenny took small steps towards *Shammai* and said, "I am very sorry. Please forgive me for doubting you."

Shammai said, "I want you to forgive me so I may be eternally among the saints."

Jenny, kissing her forehead, said, "You are a living saint."

Shammai felt light at heart. They all left the police station with the warmth of love.

